TRUCK DRIVERS
DELIVER GOODS

Photo Credits:
© Genat/Highway Images: 3, 18
© Genate/Highway Images: 20
© Grimm/Highway Images: 28
© Jack McConnell: 10, 12, 14
© Alan Levenson/Tony Stone Images: 26
© Bette S. Garber/Highway Images: 4, 8, 16, 22, 24, 30
© Mark Andrews/Ton Stone Images: cover
© 1997 Mark E. Gibson/Dembinsky Photo Assoc. Inc: 6

Library of Congress Cataloging-in-Publication Data

Greene, Carol.

Truck Drivers Deliver Goods / by Carol Greene.
p.   cm.
Summary: Describes, in simple text
and photographs, the job of a truck driver.
ISBN 1-56766-560-8 (library reinforced : alk. paper)
1. Truck driving—Juvenile literature.
2. Truck drivers—Juvenile literature.
[1. Truck drivers. 2. Occupations.] I. Title.

HE5611.G66   1998   98-3106
   388.3'24—dc21   CIP
                            AC

Copyright ©1999 by The Child's World®, Inc.
All rights reserved. No part of this book may be reproduced or utilized
in any form or by any means without written permission from the publisher.

TRUCK DRIVERS
DELIVER GOODS

By Carol Greene

The Child's World®, Inc.

SAYVILLE LIBRARY

ZOOM! ZOOM!

Look at all those trucks on the road. Where are they going? What is inside them? And who are the people who drive them?

HONK! HUMMM!

This big truck is on its way to a big city. It is bringing supplies to a store. The driver sits up high so that she can see the road. She watches out for other cars, too.

SCRATCH! SCRIBBLE!

Truck drivers must always keep track of where they are going. They must know what they are carrying, too. Some truck drivers write things down on paper. Others have **computers** inside their trucks.

BEEP! BEEP!

This truck is owned by a company that delivers packages. Some of the packages are little. Others are big brown boxes.

Each day the driver goes to the **terminal**. The trucks there are full of packages that need to be delivered. The driver is given a truck to drive for the day. He makes sure all of the packages get to where they belong.

The driver travels the same area each day.

BEEP! BEEP!

Sometimes he must drive in heavy traffic.

BEEP! BEEP!

He must watch out for children and animals, too. He must be a good and careful driver.

OOOF! THUMP!

This driver unloads a heavy package from his truck. Drivers who deliver packages must be strong and healthy.

HONK! HONK!

This driver moves many heavy things. He drives a moving van. A moving company owns the van.

"TEN-FOUR!"

A **dispatcher** at the company talks to the driver on the radio. She tells the driver where his next stop will be.

The driver pulls up to a house. A family is moving today. He helps to load up the family's belongings.

UGH!

It is hard work. The company hires other people to help him.

HONK! HONK!

Then the truck goes to another city. The driver and his helpers unload. They take everything into the family's new home.

BLAAAT!

This driver drives a huge tractor-trailer. She will go all the way across the country. A big trucking company owns her truck, too. It tells her where to go next.

Before they go anywhere, truck drivers check their trucks. Is everything working right? Has the load been put in safely?

BLAAAT!

Off goes the truck. Drivers are often gone for a week. Most of the time they drive at night. There is less traffic then.

DRIP. DRIP. SPLASH!

Sometimes drivers must drive in bad weather.

BLAAAT!

Sometimes they must drive through crowded streets. They must be very good drivers.

This driver takes a break at a **truck stop**. He calls his family to say he'll be home soon. Then—BLAAAT!—he's back on the road.

QUESTIONS AND ANSWERS

What do truck drivers do?

Truck drivers move things from one place to another. Some move things in little trucks. Others drive big tractor-trailers. Some work in just one area. Others travel around the whole country.

How do people learn to be truck drivers?

Some truck drivers learn by watching and working with other truck drivers. But the best way to learn to drive big trucks is to take a training course. Many vocational-technical schools offer these courses. Some drivers must earn a special driver's license from their state.

What kind of people are truck drivers?

Drivers must be strong, healthy people. They should be patient and good with other people. They should like to work with machines and enjoy being alone sometimes. Most of all, they should be safe, careful drivers.

How much money do truck drivers make?

Different kinds of truck drivers make different amounts of money. Some earn about $20,000 a year. Others can make over $40,000 a year. Drivers who travel long distances make the most.

GLOSSARY

computer (kom-PYOO-ter)
A computer is a special machine that holds information. It also gives answers quickly.

dispatcher (dis-PAT-chur)
A dispatcher is the person who tells truck drivers where to drive. Dispatchers sometimes use radios to talk to the drivers.

terminal (TER-mih-null)
A terminal is a building where truck drivers pick up and drop off goods. Some terminals are very large.

truck stop (TRUK STOP)
A truck stop is a place where truck drivers and other people can stop and rest. Most truck stops have restaurants and bathrooms.

INDEX

being careful, 7, 13
checking, 25
computers, 9
delivering, 11
dispatcher, 17
driving, 7, 13, 27, 29
questions and answers, 31
terminal, 11
tractor-trailer, 23
truck stop, 30
unloading, 15, 21

CAROL GREENE has published over 200 books for children. She also likes to read books, make teddy bears, work in her garden, and sing. Ms. Greene lives in Webster Groves, Missouri.

SAYVILLE LIBRARY
11 COLLINS AVE
SAYVILLE, NY 11782

KODANSHA INTERNATIONAL LTD.
Tokyo, New York & San Francisco

Christianity and Japan

Meeting ✦ Conflict ✦ Hope

Stuart D. B. Picken / Introduction by Edwin O. Reischauer

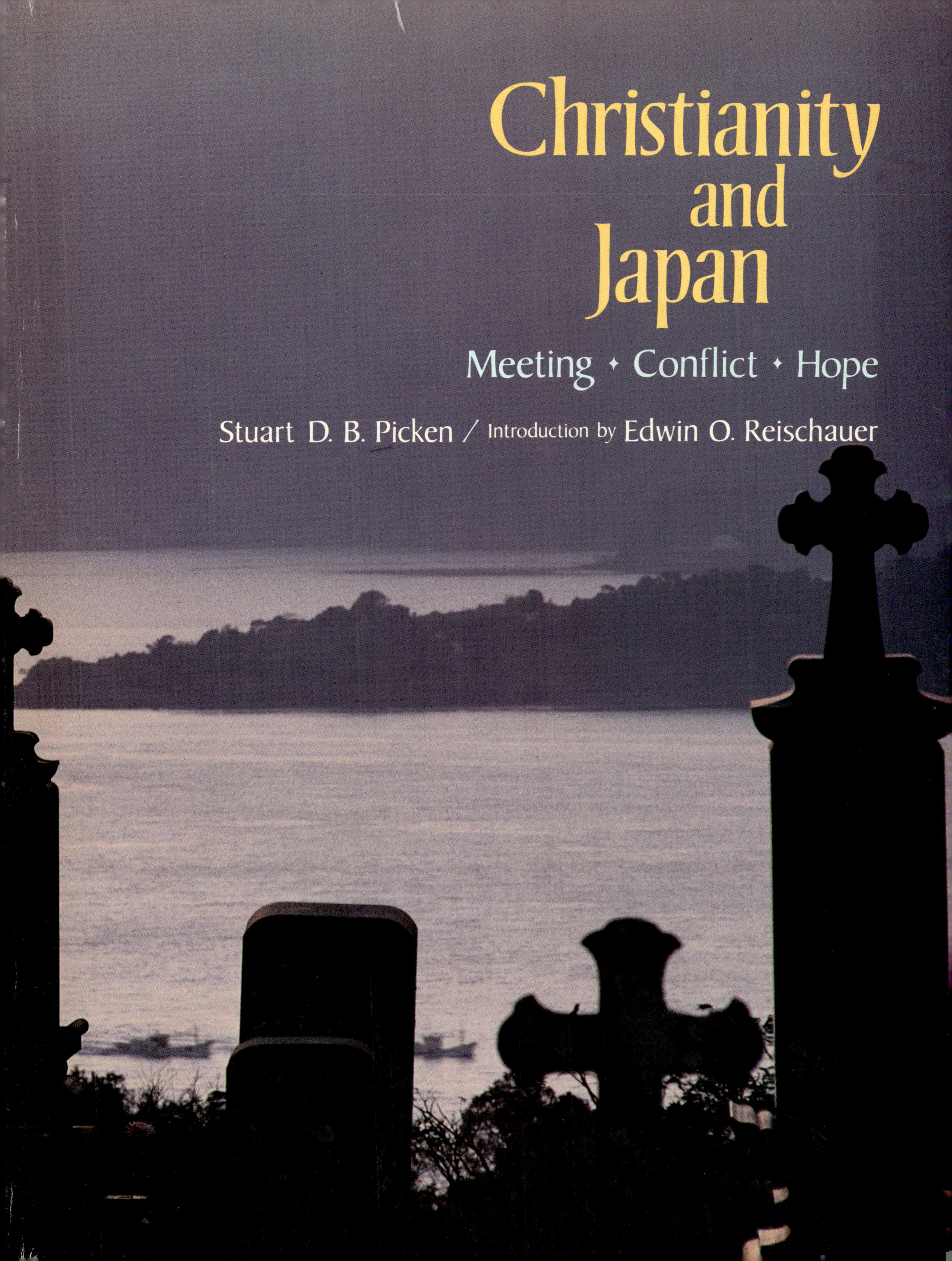

PHOTO CREDITS: (*numbers are page numbers*) Asahi Shimbun, 26–27, 46–47. Billy Graham Dendō Kyōkai, 74 (*top, bottom*). Bon Color Photo Agency, 1, 16, 34–35 (*top*). Otis Cary, 55 (*bottom*), 64. *Daily Tōhoku*, 19. Dandy Photo, 22–23. Dōshisha University, 53, 58 (*top*). 72. Fine Photo, 12, 14–15, 66 (*top*). Kyōko Grant, 70 (*bottom*). Hayashi Tadahiko, 2–3, 34 (*bottom*), 35 (*bottom*), 42–43, 59. International Christian University, 67 (*top left*), 71 (*bottom*). International Photo Press Service, 39 (*bottom*), 48, 50 (*top right, bottom left*), 51, 58 (*bottom*), 75 (*top, bottom*). Irie Taikichi, 13. Kaneko Keizō, 24, 54–55 (*top*), 66 (*bottom*), 79. Kobe City Museum, 30–31, 32, 38 (*top*). Kyoto University, 40. Makuya Kyōkai, 77. Meiji Gakuin, 68. Namban Bunkakan, 38 (*bottom*), 39 (*top*). PANA, 50 (*top left*), 70 (*top*). Rikkyō University, 67. Risshō Kōseikai, 28. Shirakawa Yoshikazu, 10–11. Tokue Akihiko, 67 (*top right, center right, bottom right and left*), 69, 71 (*top, center*). Tokyo Photo Agency, 9. Tōyō Bunko, 49. Tōyō Eiwa, 67. Tsuda Juku, 63.

Picture research and design by Katakura Nobuhiro; editorial work by Martha Tocco; maps on front and back endpapers by Kojima Michio.

Distributed in the United States by Kodansha International/USA Ltd. through Harper & Row, Publishers, Inc., 10 East 53rd Street, New York, New York 10022. Published by Kodansha International Ltd., 12–21, Otowa 2-chome, Bunkyo-ku, Tokyo 112 and Kodansha International/USA Ltd., 10 East 53rd Street, New York, New York 10022 and 44 Montgomery Street, San Francisco, California 94104. Photographs Copyright © 1983 by Kodansha International Ltd. Text Copyright in Japan 1983 by Kodansha International Ltd. All rights reserved. Printed in Japan.

LCC 82-48787
ISBN 0-87011-589-8
ISBN 4-7700-1089-3 (in Japan)

CONTENTS

Introduction *by Edwin O. Reischauer*	6
Christianity and Asian Civilization	17
Jesus of History and Christ of Faith / Changing Images / The Church of the East / Nestorius and Nestorianism / Christianity and the Japanese	
Religion and Society in Japan	20
Japanese Religiosity / Shinto: The Divine in the Natural Order / Buddhism: Reverence for Ancestors / Confucianism: Obedience and Hierarchy / Traditional Beliefs as Obstacles to Christianity / Further Obstacles	
The First Meeting	29
Francis Xavier: Missionary to the East / Xavier in Japan / A Man and a Saint / Xavier's Japanese Mission Continues	
Nagasaki: The Sea and the Cross	36
Trade and the Great Ships / Alessandro Valignano, Jesuit Visitor / City Social Structure and Mission Finance / The Jesuit Life-style / Christian Art, Japanese Artists / Valignano's Embassy to Rome	
Persecution and the Hidden Christians	41
Change of Policy / Oda Nobunaga / Toyotomi Hideyoshi / Nagasaki Martyrdom / Tokugawa Ieyasu / Toward an Edict of Persecution / Martyrdom and Apostasy / The Shimabara Rebellion / Hidden Christians / The Christian Legacy	
Meiji-Era Christian Missions	52
Japan Again Meets the Gospel / The Reemergence of the Hidden Christians / Japanese Reembrace Christianity / Niijima Jō / The Christian Bands / Japan's First Protestant Church	
Chariots of Fire	60
Japanese Christian Leadership / Intellectuals / The Social Gospel / Christian Feminism / Bridge Builders	
Mainstream Churches	65
Presbyterian and Dutch Reformed Churches / The Congregational Church / The Anglican-Episcopal Church / Methodist Episcopal / The Baptist Tradition / The Salvation Army / The Orthodox Church / The Roman Catholic Church / The Religious Bodies Law / Postwar Attitudes	
A Future of Hope	73
Common Characteristics of Church Life / The Christian Presence / Social Conscience / The Japanese Contribution to Christianity / The Christian Contribution to Japan	
Bibliography	80

INTRODUCTION

Edwin O. Reischauer

Japan is usually not considered to be a Christian country. This is natural when one looks at the statistics. Christianity probably reached its high point in the early seventeenth century, when 2 or at the most 3 percent of the population embraced the religion. Not long afterwards, even these small numbers were stamped out almost completely, and for two centuries Christianity was banned from Japan with thorough and ruthless ferocity. After it was tolerated once again not much more than a century ago, it did not regain proportionately even the modest strength it had once possessed, remaining always less than 1 percent of the population.

It may seem surprising, then, that Christianity is generally looked upon as ranking with Shinto and Buddhism as one of the three main religions of modern Japan. Its prestige is high; its influence permeates the whole country; and the average Japanese student probably could give a clearer and more accurate description of the doctrines of Christianity than of either Buddhism or Shinto. Though small in numbers, Christians occupy a disproportionately high percentage of important posts throughout society. They are strongest perhaps in the areas of education and intellectual life—several of the postwar presidents of Tokyo University, the nation's most prestigious educational institution, have been Christians—but even in politics, three of Japan's sixteen postwar prime ministers have been Christians.

An evaluation of the role of Christianity in Japan is not easy. It is made particularly difficult by the confusion between Christianity, Westernization, and modernization. The three are so intimately intertwined that no one could take them apart. To what extent is higher education for women—an area in which Christians in Japan have played a particularly important role—the result of the Christian emphasis on the worth of the individual, or of general Western attitudes toward women, or of the technical demands of modern society? In social welfare, how much has the drift toward a welfare state been the product of Christian concepts of charity, of Western ideals of equality, or of the needs of the modern urban, industrialized state?

That only a small percentage of Japanese claim to be Christians is not surprising in a country where the vast majority of the people profess no specific religion at all. The number of Christians is not so much smaller than the number who claim to be Shintoists or even Buddhists. Even among the latter two, the bulk would not claim membership in any of the long-established branches of these religions but in relatively modern offshoots from them or in syncratic sects formed out of their elements. Almost all Japanese participate in both Shinto and Buddhist rites and festivals and feel the closeness to nature that is the foundation of Shinto, but not many of them define themselves as Shintoists or Buddhists. Most Japanese show strong Confucian philosophic influences, but none would claim to be a Confucianist.

As with their older religions—Shinto, Buddhism, and Confucianism—the Japanese are able to accept Christian concepts and attitudes—and to participate in Christian rites and festivals, such as the pervasive music and decorations of the Christmas season and modish Christian-style weddings, without committing themselves to the doctrines of the religion. However appealing Christian ethics may be, many Japanese find Christian beliefs about the relationship between Christ, the man, and an all-embracing God an unsurmountable barrier to faith. It is common for Japanese intellectuals to express the desire to believe but the inability to do so.

Japan is intellectually a strongly secularized country. The people feel the subtle emotional pulls of Shinto and Buddhism and the strong intellectual appeal of Christianity and Confucianism, but relatively few of them wish to go beyond this to an unlimited commitment to faith in any of these religions. The few who do are in a sense the hard core of adherents—what we would consider in our society the devoted churchgoers even in a non-churchgoing milieu. Among these, those who respond basically to emotional needs are likely to turn to the various sectarian offshoots of

Buddhism and Shinto, while those responding to more intellectual needs may well turn to Christianity. The number of actual Christian church members should thus be considered only the core of a much larger Christian influence.

During Japan's "Catholic" century from 1549 to 1640, Christianity and the Westernization with which it was then associated were different from what they are today. So also was the feudal society the Christians found in Japan and its feeling of threat from the external loyalties Christianity bred. But one thing has not changed between then and now. In the sixteenth century the Christians dealt mainly in intellectual terms with the leading classes of Japan. This was one of the sources of dispute between the dominant Jesuits and the Franciscan friars, who preached to the underprivileged in society. When the Protestants, largely from the United States, started their missions in 1859 on the eve of the opening of the Japanese ports to trade, they too made their appeal largely in intellectual terms to the better-educated classes.

This approach was virtually forced on the Protestants by the situation they found themselves in. They were restricted to a few treaty ports, far away from the Japanese masses, but eager samurai intellectuals and would-be businessmen sought them out to learn English. The missionaries found a ready hearing for their ideas, especially among the young samurai of the areas in eastern and northern Japan which had lost out in the so-called Meiji Restoration of 1868, which was in effect a revolution that brought in a new government dominated by men from western Japan. These young samurai of the losing side found their old Confucian concepts discredited by Western technology and ideas and the road to domestic political power blocked by their rivals from other parts of Japan. They turned to the missionaries for English as a necessary tool for trade in the new age and to Christianity as an organized body of ethical concepts more in keeping with the new age than was Confucianism.

Three trends emerged from these early beginnings of the Protestant movement in Japan which have persisted ever since. One was that the samurai leadership of the new church was proud and independent, working from the start to create a fully independent Japanese Christian church. With the sympathetic aid of the more enlightened of the missionaries, they succeeded in doing this at a relatively early stage, as compared with mission fields in other Asian countries. This saved Christianity from the stigma of association with Western domination and imperialism. The Japanese leadership also sought to save Christianity in Japan from the sectarianism of the West though with less success. One leader, Uchimura Kanzō, went so far as to found a "no-church" movement, in which Christianity was passed on by university and high school teachers to their disciples without the intervention of any formal church organization. Many of Japan's intellectual leaders have stemmed from this very Japanese branch of Christianity, and one of the most prominent recent prime ministers, Ōhira Masayoshi, was a "no-church" Christian.

Another persistent trend in Japanese Christianity has been a strong emphasis on education. The early Protestant missionaries, responding to the demands of young Japanese, founded schools. These grew into important high schools in the early years of the Meiji period and into mass universities in more recent times. Christians, both missionaries and native Japanese, played a particularly large role in secondary higher education for women, a field neglected by the government.

A third trend of Christianity has been its tendency to represent a more liberal alternative path to modernization. The early Christian samurai were outsiders in the new Meiji system, and they became a part of the opposition to the government in power, as expressed through the popular press and political parties. Liberalizing trends in a heavily regimented educational system were usually of Christian inspiration. Around the turn of the century, Christians came to lead not just in social service activities but in the introduction of socialist concepts. Japan's most famous social service worker was the Christian Kagawa Toyohiko, and a Christian strain is still discernible in the Socialist party. The one postwar Socialist prime minister, Katayama Tetsu, was a man from this Christian background.

The first wave of Protestant missionaries, which started in 1859, included a number of outstanding individuals, some of whom I can remember from my childhood days, though my memories of the stalwart early samurai Christians are much sharper. This wave had largely run its course by the late nineteenth century, and there was a gap of several years before a new burst of missionary zeal in North America sent another wave to Japan in the early twentieth century.

My parents, who belonged to this second wave, illustrated well the continuing dominant trends of the Christian church in Japan. My father had gone to Japan under the Presbyterian Mission specifically for educational work, teaching at Meiji Gakuin, one of the typical missionary institutions for young men in Tokyo, and in its theological department, which, with his encouragement, developed into the independent Japan Theological School. He sympathized strongly with the policy of Japanese leadership in Christian schools, looking with deep disapproval on the missionary leadership in Christian schools in most of Asia and in some of the sects in Japan. Only briefly did he himself occupy the headship of a school, Joshi Gakuin, a socially prominent girls' school in Tokyo, and then only on a temporary basis to help out in some local school crisis. When he came to what he considered his most important work, the founding in 1918 of a full-fledged Christian women's university, the Tokyo Women's University, he persuaded a prestigious Christian intellectual and League of Nations diplomat, Nitobe Inazō, to be its first president and a Christian woman scholar, Yasui Tetsu, to be its second, while he remained in the background as an organizer and fund raiser and did liaison work with the supporting mission boards in North America.

My mother devoted her activities to the social welfare activities that had become a major strand of Christianity in Japan, working for the Women's Christian Temperance Union and various welfare programs, all headed by Japanese women. Because my sister was born deaf, my mother turned her attention to the education of the deaf, which was seriously neglected at that time in Japan. After some study in the United States, she persuaded others to join her in the founding in 1920 of the Japan Deaf Oral School, which as an innovative institution still flourishes today.

My father early realized that the simple story of Christ was not very convincing to Japanese and that they should be approached on a more intellectual level. He did not see how this could be done without knowing more about Japanese religion, and for this reason devoted himself to the study of Japanese Buddhism and to writing books about it, until he became a recognized authority on the subject. He was also resigned to the fact that Christianity was not likely to win the open adherence of many Japanese in his day but that it had already come to exercise great influence on their ideals, ethical concepts, and way of life.

On the surface Christianity in Japan may strike some people as a trifling subject, made somewhat exotic by its association with the spectacular but tragic story of the Catholic missions of the sixteenth and seventeenth centuries, but not of much significance in twentieth-century Japan. One need not penetrate very far into Japanese society, however, to perceive that Christianity is of major importance today. Though it is not easily disentangled from Westernization and modernization, there is a definitely Christian background, if not distinctively Christian form, to many of the ideals and goals of contemporary Japan. And the small band of declared Christians have a surprisingly strong influence in society. Japan is not a Christian land in the normal sense, but Christianity is an important part of Japan as it exists today.

1. Japan is a country with extreme weather variations, from the biting, dry cold of winter to the sweltering heat and torrential downpours of summer. Watsuji Tetsurō (1889–1960), a philosopher of culture, often explored in his writings the possible influence climate might have on national character and religious traditions. He identified snow with the rational mood of the northern hemisphere and bamboo with the unpredictability of the monsoon climate of the southern hemisphere. The photograph here of bamboo bending under the weight of snow symbolizes these two aspects of Japanese society. While Japan's sudden climatic shifts demand that the Japanese respond constantly to sudden changes, thus leading, perhaps, to their being described as a tolerant and adaptable people, this same ability might also account for the difficulty many Japanese have in understanding the kind of unwavering faith Christianity requires of its believers.

2. Running south along the Red Sea coast from the northern tip of the Gulf of Suez, lying inland from the coastline of the Sinai Peninsula, is the Dophkah Desert of the Old Testament. The gorgeous sunset colors painting the stark rock and sand powerfully symbolize the austerity of the Christian tradition—a tradition which grew out of Judaism which was itself rooted to this harsh soil. There is no better example of the uncompromising spirit of monotheism than the unforgiving desert. And how different from this panorama is the terrain of Japan, with its vibrant seasons, abundant flowers, and verdant forests. This divergence in natural landscape well represents the difficulty with which Christianity was transplanted from its original homeland to the Land of the Rising Sun.

3. Natural landscape does not present the only contrast between Eastern and Western values. The Western view of nature, as something to control and shape to fit the human will, contrasts sharply with the Japanese reverence for nature unadorned, deified. The Cologne Cathedral was built from stone cut, carved, and carried by human labor: an ageless fortress made by man in which to worship God. (*left overleaf*)

4. At Ōmiwa Shrine in Nara Prefecture stands this great tree, its girth encircled by a *shimenawa* or sacred rope. The tree itself is worshiped as a *kami* or divine presence. Nature untouched and nature conquered—opposite views on the expression of human spirituality. Shinto, Japan's indigenous religion, deifies the beauty of nature while Christianity often regards nature as a symbol of sinful desires. A Christianity that is truly Japanese will take into account such different attitudes toward the expression of religious sentiment. (*right overleaf*)

5. The cross atop the Xavier Memorial Catholic Church pierces the skyline of Hirado. A beautiful city nestled in a valley between hills that sweep down to the harbor, Hirado was one of the early ports of anchor for Portuguese trading ships and one of the first sites of success for Francis Xavier and his Jesuit missionary associates. In the sixteenth century Hirado came to have a large Christian population, and still today many similar church spires proclaim, against a backdrop of temple roofs, the enduring success of early Catholic missionary efforts.

CHRISTIANITY AND ASIAN CIVILIZATION

... you shall receive power when the Holy Spirit has come upon you; and you shall be my witness in Jerusalem and in all Judea and Samaria and to the end of the earth.

ACTS 1:8

Jesus of History and Christ of Faith

The words of Acts 1:8, spoken by Jesus of Nazareth after his Resurrection and before his Ascension, forecast the spread of Christianity, how it would develop from the private beliefs of a dozen frightened men whose leader was crucified into a great world movement embracing one-third of the world's population. Jesus accurately predicted that his disciples would bear witness in Jerusalem, and thereafter in Judea, and Samaria, and finally to all the world. In different eras, in different countries, Christ's witness has taken various forms. The Greek word for "witness" is *marturos*, from which the English word "martyr" is derived, and martyrdom, as a form of witness, has been particularly significant throughout the history of Christianity in Asia. Persecution by Jewish authorities made Christianity into a religion independent of Judaism; persecution by Roman authorities drove it further afield and eventually enabled it to make converts in lands far beyond Rome's sway.

As the Christian religion has spread it has come to embrace a kaleidoscope of meanings. The word "Christianity" must be used with care. It should not be taken to mean any single church denomination. Compared to Jesus of Nazareth's simple teachings of love, forgiveness, and trust in God's providence, the beliefs of churches are complicated. Churches are organized to include beliefs about Christ rather than being based purely on his teachings. Institutional forms of the main church denominations have invariably reflected the cultural settings in which they developed. The Roman Catholic church grew out of the vacuum left by the collapse of the Roman Empire, and its organizational structures reflect this—with the bishop of Rome holding "imperial" sway. The Greek Orthodox tradition emerged from a synthesis between Hellenism and near Asian culture. The Reformed and Protestant churches' emphasis on a work ethic reflects the Renaissance and the development of new centers of economic power.

Most Americans and Europeans know something about the spread of Christianity and the Roman Empire, of its division into Greek and Roman halves, and of further fragmentation at the Reformation. They are aware of the movement of Catholicism to Central and South America and of the sailing of the simple Reformed Gospel on the *Mayflower*. They know of these events as part of their cultural heritage, and so naturally do they link Christianity with the achievements of Western civilization that they tend to think of Christianity as a purely Western religion. Yet it is not inaccurate to speak also of Christianity as an Oriental religion.

Changing Images

Christianity in Asia today often looks like little more than an appendage to Western Christianity. But when the spread of Christianity is seen in the perspective of its wider development and geographical expansion throughout the ages, Christianity in Asia assumes its just importance. Christianity existed in Asia before the great Jesuit missions of the sixteenth century. Its spread was interrupted, but when it returned traces remained of what had gone before. Christianity in Asia benefits from this continuity. That there was and in the future might again be a strain of Asian Christianity that expresses Christian ideas in Asian forms is one exciting possibility latent within the volatile conditions of the late twentieth century.

6. This bride and groom, dressed in Western-style formal wear, were married in a Catholic ceremony at St. Paul's Church in Karuizawa, Nagano Prefecture. Posed for their formal wedding portrait, they are surrounded by family members, many of whom are wearing traditional Japanese wedding kimono. Standing directly behind the bride is the officiating priest, robed in traditional Catholic vestments. Japanese wedding kimono are made of silk dyed to a deep, rich black, adorned at the top with delicate white topstitching and richly ornamented at the bottom with hand-dyed or hand-painted motifs. The combination of festival raiment depicted here emphasizes the Japanese and Western melding that is one aspect of Christianity in Japan.

Christianity may have become more predominantly a Western religion, but it is a universal faith. Its future need have no geographical limits. For readers familiar with its Western development, it is helpful to understand the Eastern spread of Christianity—to see its false starts, reverses, and successes. Christianity's Eastern meeting, totally different from that in the West, provided the foundations upon which Asian Christianity was built. These same foundations support its future.

The Church of the East

The birth of the Christian church is usually dated from the Day of Pentecost (A.D. 33), the day on which the Holy Spirit came down to Peter and the other apostles. In the account given of the incident in the New Testament Book of Acts, mention is made that "Parthians and Medes and Elamites, and dwellers in Mesopotamia" were among the congregation that heard Peter preach the first sermon in Christian history (Acts 2:9). People came from the Parthian Empire, which lay beyond the eastern frontiers of Rome's imperial boundary and which, after the year A.D. 226, became part of the new Persian Empire. That empire not only rivalled Rome in size and power, but eventually, like Rome, became a Christian empire. Whereas the Christianity of the Roman Empire grew and nurtured Western civilization, the Christianity of the Persian Empire, along with its missions in India, China, and beyond, succumbed to historical pressures that destroyed it almost entirely. It was at one time a vibrant and dynamic Christianity quite different from anything we can imagine today.

These Persian Christians used the ancient Syriac language for religious writing. Wherever Syriac writing remains, therefore, we know of the existence of this religion. It maintained stout independence of thought and government from the four major theological centers of the age, Rome, Constantinople, Antioch, and Alexandria, which proselytized in Latin and Greek. Persian Christianity's dreams of mission knew no limits, and it successfully penetrated Central Asia and the Far East during the same period that the Celtic church was laying down the foundations of Christianity in the north and west of Europe. In the year A.D. 635, Bishop Aidan went from the tiny Scottish island of Iona to visit the pagan kingdom of Northumbria in England and began evangelizing the English. Contemporary with Bishop Aidan's visit is the visit of the Persian Bishop Alopen to the capital of T'ang China, where he was respectfully received by Emperor Kao Tsung. The first steps to bring Christianity to England and China were thus taking place simultaneously. How did all this begin?

Early legends abound concerning Christianity's first contacts with the East. For example, among the Syriac writings which remain there is a book called *The Acts of Thomas* in which is described the visit of the Apostle Thomas to the Indian subcontinent. And indeed, when the wandering Venetian Marco Polo made his second visit to India in 1292 he was shown a tomb alleged to be that of the martyred saint. We can most accurately date the flowering of the Church of the East from the reign of King Piroz (457–84), when Persia accepted Nestorian Christian refugees. This event has always been associated with the life of a man named Nestorius.

Nestorius and Nestorianism

In 428, Nestorius became the Patriarch of Constantinople (modern Istanbul), the equivalent of what would now be head of the Greek Orthodox Church. He preached a series of controversial sermons in defense of a presbyter who had criticized the use of the term *theotokos* (Greek meaning "God-bearer") to describe Mary, the Mother of Jesus. What began as a local issue quickly blew up into a major doctrinal dispute. Nestorius was deposed by the church council in 431 and exiled to Egypt; he died there in 451. His ideas, however, did not die, and his followers were soon being harassed by the conservative wing of the Greek church. Many of them escaped into Persia, where initially they also faced hideous persecution. Eventually, because the rivalry between Rome and Persia was so great, Persia decided to protect these Nestorian Christians. The number of these believers in Persia was large, and they were able to exert a great influence on the small band of Christians already there. This church subsequently became known as the Nestorian church, although Nestorius had little to do with its foundation, and the degree to which Nestorian teachings were followed remains unknown.

The reputation of the Nestorian church was based on its education and welfare programs. These programs were dispensed from monasticlike centers the missionaries set up as they propagated the church's teachings. Once the church had spread into Central Asia, flourishing centers of Christian activity could be found as far removed from Constantinople as Afghanistan and Tibet. This was several hundred years before Mohammed was born or the Krishna legend appeared in India.

In China all that remains of the Nestorian church is a tablet that was set into a wall in Sian in 781 describing the "Spread of the Syrian Religion in the Central Kingdom." The text itself, as the following excerpt shows, is a fascinating example of the translation of Christian ideas into the thought forms of Chinese culture:

> There is none but our wondrous Trinity, the unoriginated true Lord.
> He appointed the cross to determine the four quarters.
> He stirred up the primordial wind (spirit) and brought to life the two forces of nature (*yin and yang*).

That a description of Christ could be rendered into the ornate, symbolic style characteristic of Chinese philosophical language indicates that, to some extent at least, Christian ideas were neither wholly foreign nor unpalatable in this distant land.

But along with understanding of Christian ideas came resentment and fear of an alien faith. As had been true with Buddhism for long periods, the persecution of Christianity was inevitable, and great damage was done. The rise of Islam was followed by the Crusades, which engendered Islamic resentment of Christianity. Nestorian Christianity was felled by the Islamic backlash. Few traces of its mission further afield remain; two that do, however, indicate that it might have reached Japan.

In the *Shoku Nihongi*, a chronicle compiled by the Japanese in about 790, there is a reference to a visit made in A.D. 736 by a Persian, accompanied by three Chinese, to the court of Emperor Shōmu, who reigned from 724 to 748. It has been suggested that the Persian was a Nestorian monk. Also, in the Hōryū-ji, Japan's oldest surviving Buddhist temple, dating back to the seventh century, one of the wooden beams is carved with crosses and a written script akin to Syriac. While no substantial influence can be found, the possibility that Nestorian Christianity reached Japan at all underscores the extent to which the Church of the East stretched to fulfill its mission.

Christianity and the Japanese

Christianity and Japan are not readily associated, yet Christianity does have an image in Japan. One missionary wrote that, even when he went into an area with no church, it was obvious that someone or something had preceded him. This aura is the legacy of the sixteenth-century Catholic and the nineteenth-century Protestant missions.

Today the attitude toward Christianity in Japan is markedly ambivalent. The Japanese people generally think of Christianity as being highly ethical and difficult to understand, and this view naturally impedes Christianity's wider acceptance. But at the same time many Japanese admire Christianity for its emphasis on the "individual" and its historical and philosophical role in the evolution of Western civilization. To this must be added Christianity's continued role in widening Japanese horizons, just as early Christian missions helped Japan prepare for and feel comfortable in the modern world. Perhaps of greater significance, however, is that Christianity, more than any other source, is responsible for the growth of social concern in Japan.

To the unfolding of these themes—ambivalence, modernity, and social conscience—the remaining pages of this book are devoted.

In Heraimura, Aomori Prefecture, a cross marks a hillside grave supposed to be that of Jesus Christ. According to a legend, Jesus came to Japan after his crucifixion, married, died, and was buried in this remote area.

RELIGION AND SOCIETY IN JAPAN

Japan is a country which has unabashed doubts concerning Christianity and has confidence in its ability to live without it. In Japan, the very raison d'être of the Gospel truth itself is doubted, and the value of the existence of the church itself, rather than good or bad evangelistic methodology, questioned.

Suzuki Masahisa

Japanese Religiosity

There have been two lengthy meetings between the Japanese and Christianity, the first separated from the second by the 200 years of Japan's self-imposed isolation from the rest of the world. Continuing from 1549 until 1650, the initial meeting between the Japanese people and Catholic missionaries spanned a full century. The second Christian encounter, often referred to as the "Protestant Century," began with renewed evangelical effort in 1859 and continues to the present.

Despite encouraging beginnings, the Christian community has remained less than 1 percent of the Japanese population: Christ's religion has obviously met with effective resistance. The political circumstances surrounding both encounters combined with a general hostility to all things foreign to curtail widespread conversion of the Japanese. Organized hostility is relatively easy to document. Less obvious, but equally important, are deeply rooted Japanese attitudes, systems of values, and beliefs about the social order.

Japanese religiosity is difficult to define. If a Japanese is asked, "What's your religion?" the immediate response is often a bemused stare. This response becomes less bewildering as more is understood about how Japanese become involved in religion and what religion means in Japan.

The Japanese word for religion, *shūkyō*, means literally "sect teaching." In answer to the question "What's your religion?" the response which follows the initial stare is likely to be "I am *mushūkyō*." This is usually (but I think mistakenly) translated as "I have no religion." What I think is actually meant by this answer is that the respondent is wholly indifferent to the specific distinctions between different religious sects within Shinto and Buddhism. Still, this same person will vigorously carry and bounce the *omikoshi* (portable shrine) at a Shinto festival and beat the *taiko* drum at a Buddhist *Bon* Festival dance in memory of the ancestral spirits. He or she may be indifferent to doctrines and creeds but not indifferent to religion as an understructure for life. In Japan religion is something which binds the individual and society in meaningful unity. This aspect of Japanese religiosity has often been neglected, yet it is one of the most powerful barriers to the development of Christianity in Japan.

Let us look closely at the three major elements of Japanese religiosity.

Shinto: The Divine in the Natural Order

Japan is intricately crisscrossed by a network of some 100,000 Shinto shrines signifying devotion to the *kami*—those awe-inspiring phenomena of nature which express divine being. Every Japanese is under the protection of one of these shrines, the oldest of which predate written history. At great events like New Year celebrations, more than eighty million Japanese visit these shrines, donate large amounts of money as offerings, and pray for good fortune and success. Worshipers receive protection in the form of purification; nowadays anything from an automobile to a baseball team may be purified.

Along with ritual purification, the old agricultural festivals continue both in rural areas and, with modifications, in the city as well. Indeed, these festivals are one occasion when otherwise restrained and polite Japanese behave with complete unselfconscious spontaneity. Japanese react sensitively to places that have a holy atmosphere, and shrines, which are places and not buildings, are predominantly located in picturesque spots because the Japanese people have a deep affinity for natural beauty. I knew of a Tokyo man (reputedly *mushūkyō*) who, before going to the United States for a year's study, flew to his family shrine in faraway Kyushu at great cost simply to pick up a pebble from the shrine grounds as a talisman. When he returned safely to Japan, he flew again to Kyushu to replace the pebble. That may not be religious faith as Westerners understand it. But it is one variety of Japanese religious devotion—dependence upon the divine character of the natural order.

Buddhism: Reverence for Ancestors

Flowing alongside the Shinto reverence for the divine in the natural order is the Buddhist reverence for one's ancestors. Japanese Buddhism, which instills and encourages respect for ancestors, is not the Buddhism of India. Buddhism was introduced to Japan from China where it had undergone many modifications of the original Indian beliefs. Chinese Buddhism incorporated a strong belief in ancestor reverence. Although Japanese Buddhism came to have its own distinct characteristics, it retained a close concern for ancestors. As an outgrowth of this, Buddhism is responsible for Japanese funeral customs, and control of the funeral remains an important factor in maintaining people's bonds to the old faith.

The Japanese reverence for ancestors, and for the dead in general, is a powerful factor in Japanese religiosity. The designation of an *ikibotoke* (a living Buddha), the tradition of revering someone during his lifetime for a great religious feat, demonstrates the depth of this devotion. Since the word *hotoke*, which literally means "Buddha," is used colloquially to mean "the deceased," it implies that the highest honor to be paid to the living is to treat them as though they were dead. Many of the various ceremonies that surround ancestor reverence, such as visits to graves, are still practiced. Making and selling Buddhist family altars for the household, for example, is big business. These altars range in price from $200 to over $2,000, and in rural areas over 80 percent of the homes have one. Loyalty to ancestors reinforces the status quo and may account for the general resistance in Japan to foreign things, whether in theology or marketing.

Beyond encouraging ancestor reverence, Buddhism has also helped enrich Japanese social psychology in ways that are still notably visible. Traditional Buddhist doctrine taught several conditions of existence which were translated, not only into Japanese language and thought, but also into behavioral attitudes. The two main principles are those of impermanence (*mujō*), symbolized best by the cherry blossom that begins to fade as soon it has reached full bloom, and self-is-illusion (*muga*), an absolute denial of the Western philosophy of individualism. These principles have encouraged the Japanese to reject individualism in favor of group participation as the core of human identity. While the strong Japanese preference for group identification probably originated elsewhere, the influence of Buddhism has certainly helped keep it alive.

Buddhism, Japan's cultural identity, and Shinto,

World-famous martial artist Nakayama Masatoshi leads members of the Japan Karate Association in a ritual pilgrimage to Meiji Shrine, Tokyo, in 1964. In Japan, physical and spiritual strength go hand in hand, and both are consistent with belief in the natural well-being of the universe, in part a Shinto notion. Many martial arts groups are, at the same time, rigidly Confucian in organization.

7. The power and energy of Shinto is admirably displayed in its festivals (*matsuri*). Purification is a central theme and here supporters of the local Shinto shrine are boisterously carrying the portable *mikoshi* containing the spirit of the *kami* on their shoulders to dip it in the sea. Salty ocean water is believed to have the strongest purifying power. Pictured is the *hadaka matsuri*

("bare body festival") of the Tamasaki Shrine in Ichinomiya, Chiba Prefecture. This festival takes place around the middle of September and is one of the many exuberant autumn festivals. Participation in this, and indeed in every Shinto festival, is one of the uniting forces of community life and is the responsibility of both children and adults.

Japan's spiritual roots, complement each other: the one concerned with death and the other with life. This tolerant relationship has enabled them to exert religious influence over the centuries, and they, in turn, have been reinforced by Japan's rigidly hierarchic social structure.

Confucianism: Obedience and Hierarchy

Japanese rulers over the centuries have considered that the well-being of their people called for strict social management. This has meant instituting and enforcing a system of social ethics that stressed the virtues of loyalty, obedience, and respect for superiors. This system was based on the teachings of the Chinese philosopher Confucius (551–479 B.C.). Confucian philosophy spread to Japan about the same time as Buddhism, and its influence gained strength from the late sixteenth century when Confucianism was adopted by the military rulers who were then seeking to consolidate their power.

Japanese Confucianism altered the original hierarchy of relationships which had placed the father-son relationship at the top. In Japan the ruler-subject relation became the highest. The Japanese society that emerged under the influence of the victorious Tokugawa family of rulers, from 1600 until the mid-nineteenth century, was steeped in these principles. Japanese to this day consider that hierarchic relationships are the natural expression of order, and in everything from martial arts clubs and gangster mobs, to businesses, academic schools of thought, and the teaching of traditional flower arrangement, relationships are conducted on the basis of junior (*kōhai*) to senior (*sempai*) status: juniors obey seniors. There is also the *oyabun/kobun* relationship: the relation of a patriarchal godfather to the group he leads.

Traditional Beliefs as Obstacles to Christianity

A young person who desires to become a Christian may often find that these lingering feudal structures make conversion difficult. The values of Confucian ethics which decry public "loss of face" pose a barrier to the Christian values of forgiveness; it is preferable to commit suicide than to live with shame. These values also compel others to base their behavior on loyalty to their superiors. Buddhism and Confucianism for centuries have actively promoted national unity and social harmony. The Japanese people have been encouraged to prefer harmony to conflict, negotiation to confrontation. The religious spirit embodied in the commandment "You shall have no other gods before me" could be viewed as a potential threat to social harmony.

Japanese culture is very highly developed, and there are few avenues by which a new religion can enter. Tradition offers resistance to religious innovation. Value systems evolve as civilization evolves: they are at once the product and producer of tradition. They take centuries to develop and resist sudden change, for their function is to give order, meaning, and purpose to society and its institutions. Value systems include the beliefs, rules, and ideals embraced by a people and enable their understanding of and outlook on life. Traditional values, in Japan as elsewhere, function as a force for stability. At times of external upheaval they have helped Japan undergo seemingly radical change while maintaining essential continuity. Japanese values have evolved from, and in turn support, stability and order—and they continue to perform this role. Traditions interlock with the Japanese complex value system to provide the greatest, but most silent, resistance to Christianity.

Further Obstacles

Several other factors which have impeded the development of Christianity in Japan must be mentioned briefly. First, there is no philosophical basis in the

The fan is for good business, the string-drum is for good luck, and the kite is to ward off fires. These and other charms sold at Shinto shrines are aspects of a folk religion that continues to thrive in an industrial society.

Japanese system of thought for the idea of the transcendence of God. God, uncreated Creator, who stands above and beyond human activity, differs from the Japanese *kami*, who are various, immanent, and human. Japanese traditional roots are particularistic, and a universal idea, such as God's transcendence, is difficult to explain.

Second, a profound distrust of organized religion continues to exist in Japan. For 300 years, Buddhist priests functioned, in effect, as part of a network of government control. Shinto, too, was made a state religion in the Meiji period and was used to foster militaristic ideology. Christianity—which is both alien and organized—is also distrusted.

Third, the so-called "new religions," such as Sōka Gakkai or Risshō Kōseikai, have preempted some of Christianity's appeal by stressing love and friendship toward outcasts and the common people. Although these religions are often referred to as "new," they are simply old religions in revamped forms. They have not abandoned the ideals of Japan's most popular Buddhist text, the *Lotus Sutra*, nor have they disavowed reverence for ancestors. They remain totally, firmly, and traditionally Japanese, and indeed, they even incorporate a deeply Shinto outlook in their principle of *gense riyaku*, that is, the ideal of happiness achieved in this lifetime.

Fourth, Christian churches in Japan are often more concerned with orthodoxy than with the relevance of Christianity to society. Japanese Christian thinkers have made few serious attempts to concern themselves with the role Christianity can or must play in Japanese society. This was true of the sixteenth-century Jesuits and the nineteenth-century Protestants, and it is true of today's Japanese Christians as well.

All of these obstacles are by themselves powerful. To them must be added one more, one that arises out of excessive concern for orthodoxy; namely, that Japanese Christianity is too intellectual. There is no Christianity for non-intellectuals. "Deliver Japanese theology from Germanic captivity," pleaded one young Japanese theologian. The problem, however, is not merely the influence of German theology, but an attitude of reverence toward German theologians, paralleled by a similar reverence toward German philosophers. This reverence is combined with an anxiety to understand theological writings "correctly," a point of view oriented toward textual debate. Spontaneity is viewed as a threat to orthodoxy. This type of intellectual Christianity, with its long sermons delivered in the style of a lecture, is typical of many Protestant religious services and is as much a barrier there to understanding Christianity as it is to Christianity's further penetration of Japanese society. This approach is more likely to produce apostates than converts. Christ, in Japanese preaching today, is either the worshiped object of Pietism or a deified sage, the symbol of all good educators, philosophers, and reformers. In this way, Christianity becomes a form of Gnosticism, a type of superior knowledge. This ignores Christianity as a belief in "truth," as a commitment to and trust in the hope it inspires.

From the time Buddhism first appeared in Japan until the time when it became naturalized and accepted about six hundred years elapsed. Over the course of that time, Buddhism often evidenced a real willingness to incorporate aspects of Japanese society and culture into its doctrine. To be accepted, Christianity, too, must abandon intellectual elitism and become a naturalized part of Japanese society.

The Buddhist family altar is the center for devotions in memory of ancestors. The Japanese Buddhist funeral hearse is a good example of the adaption of an old form to a new one.

8. Not only the beauty of the Japanese countryside, but the Confucian heritage of respect and deference which permeates Japanese society are captured in this photograph of a chance meeting between a community member and the local Buddhist priest as both are walking along a path through a neighborhood field. Although this picture was taken in Nara Prefecture, the seat of one of Japan's oldest imperial capitals and one of the oldest centers of Buddhist activity as well, this kind of meeting is a daily event throughout Japan. (*preceding page*)

While Christianity in Japan today sometimes suggests the "modern" outlook, Japan's ancient, traditional faiths have also evolved in response to the pressures of today's world. Tenri-kyō, founded by the charismatic woman Nakayama Miki in the nineteenth century, is a modern Japanese religion that has appropriated numerous Shinto elements. Its simple and practical teachings have made it a religion of the masses. Pilgrimage to the holy city of Tenri in Nara Prefecture is one typical element of devotion, and in the photo at right are seen worshipers massing near Tenri-kyō headquarters to mark the ninetieth anniversary of the faith's establishment. Risshō Kōsei-kai, begun in 1938 by Niwano Nikkyō and now boasting 5 million adherents, is derived from the Buddhist Nichiren tradition and stresses perfection of the individual through devotion to the altruistic way of the Bodhisattva. Its headquarters, shown below, are in Western Tokyo.

28 CHRISTIANITY AND JAPAN

THE FIRST MEETING

We shall never find among heathens another race equal to the Japanese.

Francis Xavier

Francis Xavier: Missionary to the East

The personality of St. Francis Xavier and his successful evangelism in the East will always be considered remarkable. He is unique: as much a part of the history of Christianity in the West as of Christianity in the East. That the first meeting between Christianity and Japan took place at all was due to the religious zeal of Francis Xavier.

Xavier was a descendant of the ancient royal family of Navarre. A Basque Spaniard, he took his name from the castle of the town in which he was born. The date of his birth is accepted to be 7 April 1506. He was a product of his age, strictly reared according to the religious and educational characteristics of early-sixteenth-century Europe. During his studies in Paris, he became the friend of a fellow Basque, Ignatius of Loyola. Ignatius introduced Xavier to the religious ideals which were to lead to the foundation of the Society of Jesus (Jesuits) by Ignatius, Xavier, and others in 1539, two years after Xavier was ordained to the Catholic priesthood.

From its inception, foreign missionary work was a central part of the Jesuit order. Thus, Xavier was quick to respond to King John III of Portugal's appeal for a missionary to go to India. On 7 April 1541, Xavier embarked on a voyage to India to begin missionary work among the people of Goa. He left Portugal bearing papal briefs from Rome that gave him special authority to maintain and extend the faith in the Orient. Xavier was to exercise this authority with compassionate zeal.

Xavier's missionary activities took him from Goa through southern India to Ceylon and Malacca. In 1547, a vessel from China docked at Malacca and from it disembarked a Japanese named Yajirō. This man became Xavier's first Japanese convert to the gospel of Christ. Yajirō came from Kagoshima on the island of Kyushu and part of the domain of one of Japan's oldest and strongest samurai families, the Shimazu family. Xavier and Yajirō became friends, and Xavier began to teach him about Christianity. When Xavier suggested that Yajirō and his companions go to Goa for further instruction and training, they complied and were duly baptized there. Xavier's experience with Yajirō made him wish to go to Japan to preach the Gospel.

Xavier set sail for Japan in April 1549, accompanied by Yajirō, two of Yajirō's friends, and two Spanish Jesuits (Cosme de Torres and Juan Fernández). The drama that would surround Xavier's encounter with Japan began on this voyage. Because Xavier wanted to go directly to Japan, he passed up several vessels taking less direct routes in favor of a Chinese junk whose captain promised to make a direct trip. This junk turned out to be a pirate ship, sailing on a mission of plunder, but it was blown off course and, on 15 August 1549, forced to seek anchorage at Kagoshima —the birthplace of Yajirō. Xavier's prayer was dramatically answered, his missionary work in Japan auspiciously begun.

Xavier in Japan

Xavier was—and throughout his life remained—impressed with the Japanese people. The daimyō, or ruling military lord, of Satsuma, Shimazu Takahisa, received Yajirō; Yajirō, in turn, introduced Xavier. Xavier was initially welcomed to the Satsuma domain, and by the end of the year as many as 150 persons had been baptized in Kagoshima. Resentment by Buddhist priests led to Xavier's subsequent departure from Satsuma and the relocation of his missionary effort to the north in Hirado. There, Xavier's effectiveness and the number of Catholic converts continued to grow.

Inspired by the success of his mission, Xavier decided to journey to Kyoto to the north and east in the hope of being able to convert the Japanese emperor. In October of 1550, he set off with Brother Fernández and two Japanese Christians; Father Torres remained in Hirado. They stopped at Yamaguchi on

9. Imaginative embellishments combine with literal depiction in this representative *Namban byōbu* ("Southern Barbarian screen painting"), part of the collection at the Kobe City Museum. These large paneled screens, some signed by famous painters of the Kanō school of classical painting, are thought by scholars of art history to have been produced between 1590 and 1630. Accurately recording Japanese amazement at the first cultural intrusion of the West, *Namban byōbu* share several elements of typical composition. In the lower right-hand section often Jesuit priests and students will appear dressed in flowing black robes. Behind the black-robed figures may stand two Jesuit brothers dressed in gray robes, and an elderly lay-catechist leaning on a

walking stick. On the left-hand side of the screen will be a detailed depiction of a Portuguese trading ship filled with exaggeratedly tall foreign merchants and sailors of many different races. The ships will be shown stocked with exotic gifts, tigers, and rare birds, presents for the various daimyō in whose domains the ships were allowed to harbor and where foreign trade was permitted.

Classical representations of Japanese houses and landscapes often appear in the upper right section of the screen. Sometimes religious ceremonies, such as the Catholic Mass or Confession or religious instruction, appear wreathed in clouds across the top. These screens are sumptuously painted and are invaluable both as art and as social history.

THE FIRST MEETING 31

their way to Kyoto, but after four weeks of unsuccessful mission work continued on their journey. They suffered greatly in the bitter winter conditions; they trudged through deep winter snows hazarding sickness and danger and finally arrived in Kyoto in February 1551. Usually a two-week trip, the missionaries' winter journey had taken four times as long. The Kyoto endeavor proved to be a disappointment. Civil war was raging, the capital was deserted, the city was badly damaged. Xavier requested permission for an imperial audience, but the offering necessary for the granting of his request far exceeded Xavier's means. He felt that his efforts in Kyoto were useless and reluctantly decided to retrace his steps to Yamaguchi.

On the trip back, Xavier began to rethink his entire approach. When he was in India, Xavier had lived and preached among the poor as if he were poor himself. He realized that in Japan the tattered robe he wore was seen not as a symbol of the Jesuit's self-imposed poverty, but rather as evidence of his low rank. Xavier changed his approach. He sent to Hirado for a new robe and, when finely dressed, made such a favorable impression on the daimyō of Yamaguchi that he was permitted to begin preaching. His enthusiasm is obvious in his correspondence from this period:

> Though my hairs are already become all hoary, I am more vigorous than I ever was. . . . I have not in the course of all my life received a greater satisfaction than at Yamaguchi, where multitudes of people come to hear me by the ruler's permission.

The positive results of the Jesuit mission in Japan encouraged Xavier to continue his mission to Asia. Therefore, he decided to leave Japan and take the Christian message to China. On his way there, he first set sail in September 1551 for Bungo, in what is now Ōita Prefecture, Kyushu. In Bungo Xavier was received by the daimyō Ōtomo Yoshishige. On this occasion a formal procession was organized and Xavier, finely dressed, made a profound impression. Ōtomo provided positive support for Xavier's mission in Bungo. Conversions were numerous, and he spent considerable time baptizing new converts. Near the end of November 1551, after a morning spent in taking formal leave of the daimyō, Xavier finally boarded the ship that was to take him on his journey to China. Several months after he left, Xavier wrote to Loyola, "[Japan] is the only country yet discovered in these regions where there is hope of Christianity permanently taking root."

Xavier had spent a little more than two years establishing the first meeting between Christianity and the Japanese. In this short time he left an indelible impression on both the history of Japan and the history of Christianity. The results of his contribution extend to the present day.

A Man and a Saint

Francis Xavier never reached China. He became ill on the final stage of his journey and died on 2 December 1552 on a little island thirty miles southwest of Macao. Because of his active life and lonely death, a great deal of romanticism has grown up around his name. A more sober, contemporary estimate of Xavier might consider his human, as well as saintly, qualities.

While Xavier has been criticized for ignoring Japanese religions and religious beliefs, he and almost all Christians in the sixteenth century believed that salvation was not possible outside the Christian faith. Xavier, therefore, saw Japanese religion as a device of the devil—something to be overthrown. What continues now to commend Xavier to a place in history, as well as in our affections, is his zeal and enthusiasm, the humanity he showed to other human beings. His theology may have been the rigid theology of the sixteenth century—but he was practical where others were simply fanatical; he displayed consideration and understanding where others were intolerant and unforgiving. Xavier embodied the same single-minded zeal associated with St. Paul. He was one of those great-hearted religious pioneers who lived what St. Paul meant when he declared, "Woe is me if I preach not the Gospel."

Europeans preparing their departure for Asia—an orientalized portrayal by Kanō Naizen, a sixteenth-century Japanese artist. Xavier and other Catholic missionaries were objects of curiosity as well as bearers of spiritual tidings.

Xavier's Japanese Mission Continues

After Xavier left Japan, Father Torres and Brother Fernández continued his work at Yamaguchi. In late 1551, another wave of civil war broke out. During this period, 2,000 converts were baptized in the face of strong opposition from Zen and Nichiren Buddhist priests. Yet, conversions took place even among Buddhist priests, especially Zen priests. The Zen priests' high level of personal discipline enabled them to appreciate the deep religious commitment of the Jesuit missionaries, their tremendous conviction, and their dedication. In 1557 Yamaguchi was again plunged into turmoil, and again peace was restored. But in this period of relative calm, Christianity was permitted less and less freedom.

How is the progress of Christianity in a country as foreign as Japan explained? According to missionary reports, there were 30,000 Japanese converts baptized by 1570. By 1582, this number had increased to 130,000 in the Kyushu area and to 200,000 around Kyoto. Various figures have been claimed: the *Relacão Anual* of 1605 recorded that there were about 750,000 baptized persons. The most reliable sources estimate the total to have been close to 300,000, or about 2 percent of the population at that time. Christianity spread at a more rapid rate in sixteenth-century Japan than at any other time or in any other nation in Asia, and the spread of Christianity continued into the early years of the seventeenth century.

The explanation for the early success of Christianity is a complicated one. Xavier's arrival coincided with a period of enormous upheaval. The ruling Ashikaga shogunate in Kyoto was in decline; Japan was politically unstable as war lords battled for control; social and cultural development were in flux. Buddhism, while powerful and often menacing, had not developed as Japan's central religious authority. Shinto was not able to assert any strong claim to political influence because of the decline in imperial power. It was a confusing age, one of great uncertainty, without a clear, effective central authority.

That sophisticated and powerful daimyō encouraged the proclamation of an alien religion indicates not only the weakness of central authority but also the allure of steady foreign trade. For trade meant wealth. Ambitious daimyō saw a source of income in trade with the Portuguese, and many of them were eager to secure it. The Japanese had some foreign experience with the Portuguese traders who made their annual trip to Japan. It was clear that these traders held the Jesuits in high regard and followed them in matters of religious observance. The Jesuits' religious leadership in the foreign community was beyond dispute, and the respect and deference paid them by the traders provided a model for the Japanese.

The degree to which the Japanese understood the reason behind the regard in which the Jesuits were held is unclear. Some of the Japanese people considered them to be *Tenjikunin*, or itinerant monks from India. The title was given to wandering Buddhist priests who were usually considered to be magicians or miracle workers. Initially, the earliest Jesuits were probably thought to be Buddhist priests of a variety of Buddhism that had not yet come to Japan. This may be one reason why the Christian message was not rejected out of hand.

Perhaps the best explanation for Xavier's eager reception is the general mood of the time. Amidst uncertainty and lack of hope, the Japanese people might have been looking for a different view of life. Christianity's greatest single contribution is undoubtedly its location of the dignity of human life at the axis of all thought: this is the basis for the Christian social conscience. While the sixteenth century and the twentieth century differ enormously, the human spirit remains the same. The Japan of Xavier's time was chaotic and disillusioned; it was an age ready to receive a foreign religion. Christianity brought a message of hope and mercy. This message may have been Christianity's strongest point of attraction to its hearers. It may still be.

A memorial in Yamaguchi commemorates the work of Francis Xavier.

THE FIRST MEETING 33

34 CHRISTIANITY AND JAPAN

10. Outside the restored Urakami Catholic Church stand the charred statues of Catholic saints disfigured in the blast of the atomic bomb dropped on Nagasaki. These statues are a grim reminder of the horror of atomic devastation. (*left*)

11. Anyone who has ever visited Nagasaki has invariably made a pilgrimage to the famous Peace Park and paused in thought before this commemorative statue entitled "Prayer for Peace." The statue's eyes are closed in respect for the victims of the bombing; the left hand is outstretched in peace, the right pointed in warning toward the disaster that rained from the skies. Sculpted by Kitamura Seibō, this statue is a mute, powerful messenger for peace. (*below left*)

12. The city of Nagasaki is itself a testimony to the human spirit's triumph over adversity beyond comprehension. Fishing boats unload their catch at one of Nagasaki's many inlets—as they have for over four hundred years. (*below*)

NAGASAKI: THE SEA AND THE CROSS

All of us . . . considered it very necessary that we should take charge of the port of Nagasaki which is in the fief of Dom Bartholomew, and whither the Great Ship normally comes. The place is a natural stronghold, and one which no Japanese lord could take by force. Moreover, since it is the port whither the Great Ship comes, anyone who is lord of the land will be delighted to have the padres there.

Alessandro Valignano

Trade and the Great Ships

Today the bustling, international seaport of Nagasaki has a population of about 500,000. Amidst grotesque reminders that Nagasaki was the epicenter of the second atomic bomb exist undamaged zones which retain much of the city's Christian-era charm. Still to be seen today are the restored Ōura Church, the oldest in Japan, and many old foreign residences. Another visible reminder of the sixteenth century is Nagasaki's relatively large Christian population, at 4.5 percent of the total proportionately the largest of any city in Japan. Nagasaki's Catholic heritage dates back to 1567. The city was Japan's first Christian community and was the first piece of Japanese territory ceded to the Society of Jesus. Before looking at the history of the spread of Christianity in Nagasaki, we should look first at an important event which preceded it: the arrival of the Portuguese traders.

From around 1544, Prtuguese trading ships began to sail for Japan. These ships were in the six- to eight-hundred-ton class and were called *nao* ("carrack") in Portuguese and *kurofune* ("black ship") in Japanese. Merchant ships set sail from Lisbon and reached Goa six months later; sailing from Goa to Japan via Macao, after waiting out the winter, took at least another year. Including delays for the winter season and the weather, the trip from Lisbon to Nagasaki thus took two years or more. The principal items exchanged in the trade were Chinese silk for Japanese silver. Chinese silk sold in Japan for up to four times its original price. Since the trade was lucrative for all who successfully engaged in it, it is easy to understand why many Japanese daimyō were eager to profit from the taxes levied on it.

Ōmura Sumitada, the local daimyō whose domain included Nagasaki, was the first daimyō in Japan to convert to the new faith. He did so in 1563 and subsequently gave permission in 1570 for the port to be developed. Portuguese ships were anchoring at Kagoshima, but this had not proved completely satisfactory. Nagasaki—the name means "long cape," and a brief look at a map will show why—was just what the Portuguese wanted most: a safe, potentially fortifiable harbor that could be their center of trade.

In 1567, when Luis de Almeida began missionary work there, Nagasaki was a small and unimportant village. One year later veteran missionary Gaspar Vilela (1525–72) joined the effort in Nagasaki, and by the spring of 1571 a section of forest foothill land had been cleared to make way for a town of some size behind the houses of the village fishermen that were clustered around the harbor. The church was built in front of a plaza and the surrounding community was divided into six wards. In that same year when ship captain Tristao Vaz da Veiga was allowed to dock at Nagasaki, the importance of that city as both a flourishing port and Christian community was established.

Alessandro Valignano, Jesuit Visitor

When Alessandro Valignano (1539–1606) arrived as the Jesuit Visitor to Japan in 1579, Nagasaki was a city of about 400 houses and Japan's Christian converts totaled almost 100,000. Yet he was arriving at a time when the Catholic mission itself was disillusioned and when some farseeing analysis and administrative talent of the sort that Valignano could provide were sorely needed.

Valignano had spent the five years prior to his arrival in Japan as the Jesuit Visitor to India. During that time he had received reports of the progress of the Japan mission. Valignano expressed, in his views on the progress of the mission in Japan, that he considered it important, not only for missionaries, but for all Christians, to conform to local customs and attitudes and to recognize local prejudices. Valignano also believed that native Japanese should be ordained to the priesthood. In support of his belief in the need for a Japanese clergy, he established Jesuit seminaries where Japanese candidates could study for the priesthood along with European colleagues.

Valignano offered sound advice on Japanese customs and habits. He had the ability to grasp the nature of a situation immediately and could map out strategy with intuitive vision. He had great insight into the Japanese character, the state of Japanese society, the problems of Christianity, and its future in Japan. Consistent with his thinking, he warned strongly about avoiding any kind of involvement in local politics; such involvement could lead to a Christian show of force. He was correct in cautioning that such behavior might endanger the liberty and successes that had been won by the mission.

City Social Structure and Mission Finance

Under instructions from the Christian daimyō Ōmura Sumitada, non-Christians were forbidden to live in Nagasaki without church permission. Impoverished refugees from other areas of Japan were, however, allowed to settle there, and for a time this port city became a harbor of peace amidst the turmoil, chaos, and violence of the age. Nagasaki's social organization was in fact without precedent in Japanese history. Elders were elected from the body of citizens to handle civic affairs, and various institutions were organized to care for the sick and the poor. Neither heavy taxation nor severe punishment was imposed as a method of controlling the population, as it frequently was elsewhere in Japan. In the early days of the city's development probably not more than a thousand people lived there, but by 1585 reports indicate large numbers of new arrivals, and from among these came more than three hundred baptisms a year. These early days were prosperous. General and spiritual well-being, for a short time at least, existed side by side.

Ōmura Sumitada then went one step further and, in an effort to keep the lucrative Portuguese trade within his domain, offered to donate the port of Nagasaki and its neighboring village of Mogi to the Society of Jesus as a means of financing the missionary effort. Valignano, for whom mission finances were a constant concern, recognized the tremendous importance that the revenue of the trading port could have for the Jesuit mission. Many wealthy individuals had given support to the mission, and land or buildings had even been received from a few daimyō. Aid had also come from Portugal and from Rome. But the funds for the mission's various charities and other activities needed constant replenishment. After consultation with other missionaries in Japan, Valignano accepted an agreement with Ōmura and in 1580 sent it on for approval by the Jesuit General.

The terms enabled the Jesuits to charge a rental fee on trading ships anchored in the Nagasaki port. While the Jesuits would not be directly involved in the trade they would still be able to benefit from it.

This economic aid certainly helped the church to grow in Japan. By the end of 1580 there were 150,000 Christians and 200 congregations led by 85 Jesuit priests, 20 Japanese brothers, and 100 catechists. By 1590 there were 136 Jesuits and 170 catechists and approximately 180,000 converts. The missionaries and Christians of Nagasaki expanded their activities in the fields of social work, medical attention, and education, with particular emphasis on the welfare of the poor and the outcast. Much time and effort and prayer were, of course, devoted to increasing the number of Christian believers, and the growth of benevolent activities also spurred the growth of the Christian community.

The Jesuit Life-style

The Christian mission in Japan benefited from the clear guidelines Valignano set down for how the Jesuits should live. Propriety of dress and language, minimal gesticulation, suppression of laughter and temperamental displays of feeling in public were all part of the Jesuit code of behavior.

Residences were plainly but adequately designed and furnished in a Japanese style, and each priest had a room to himself which was equipped with a bedding roll, chair, table, and candle. Rooms had to be cleaned twice weekly by the occupant, although on other days his associate catechist or other servant could do the work. Other orders later criticized the Jesuits for extravagance and for having too many servants. Perhaps they became carried away with the Japanization of their missionary effort. Reports indicate only that they lived well, but not luxuriously. The Jesuits were advised to be extremely circumspect in their behavior toward the local community: strict care was taken not to arouse hostility, crosses were not to be erected without permission, and the Gospel was to be preached in such a way that European manners and customs were not introduced along with it. The basic rule was that Japanese customs were not to be interfered with except where they came into direct conflict with Christianity, and even then, rebukes should be administered gently, preferably by a Japanese brother.

Christian Art, Japanese Artists

An indirect influence of the missionary effort in Nagasaki, as well as elsewhere in Japan, was the development of Japanese Christian art. Among the items the Jesuits had brought with them were altar pictures, typically scenes from the Bible or stories of Catholic saints. So taken were the Japanese with the lavish beauty of the European paintings that after a while imported works could not fill the demand. In 1583 Father Giovanni Niccolo arrived at Nagasaki to

13. Although the cross which adorns this bowl has long been the most basic of decorative motifs found in many different cultures, this bowl is thought to have been used in Japan in Catholic religious ceremonies, perhaps as a water container for baptisms.

14. The cylindrical, lacquered box with mother-of-pearl inlay is a Host Box in which wafers for Holy Communion were stored. The inscription "IHS" is composed of the first three Greek letters in Jesus' name and is the emblem of the Jesuit Order, the first and most successful of the Catholic orders to send missionaries to Japan.

Christianity prompted not only new Japanese design motifs but new modes of craftsmanship. The objects on these pages date from around the period of Christian influence in the late sixteenth century.

15. This stand, bearing the same inscription, "IHS," is also of lacquer and mother-of-pearl. It was used as a stand for the missal during Catholic Mass.

16. These sword guards are engraved with the religious symbols of the wearer. The left and right sword guards are inscribed with crosses symbolic of the Catholic faith. The swastikalike design on the middle guard is found in many cultures and has long been associated with Buddhism.

NAGASAKI: THE SEA AND THE CROSS 39

teach European-style religious painting. Works depicting Christian themes—but painted by Japanese artists working in an unfamiliar medium—were produced in sizable numbers in Nagasaki up until about 1613.

Another Japanese school of art developed during this period which reflected the European cultural intrusion into Japan as much as its religious influence. This school of art is called the *Namban* school, and the word is loosely applied to any art painted during the period of Europe's first encounter with Japan that reflects a European theme or artistic style. In Japanese, *Namban* means "Southern Barbarian"; the men from western Europe had arrived on Japan's shores from the south. The *Namban* school of art includes works of Japanese artistry which used thoroughly traditional painting techniques to portray European dress and customs.

Among the most important artistic works of the period were the *Namban byōbu*, large folding-screen paintings embodying themes of the "Southern Barbarians." The most renowned screens were painted by masters of the greatest art school—the Kanō school of painting. What is most commonly depicted on these screens is the arrival of the Portuguese ships and the procession of disembarkation including merchants and black sailors bringing presents of Arabian horses, tigers, and other exotic items. Other screens depict the world according to the cartographical artwork being done then in Europe. Significantly, the details of Japan and China on these screens were accurate, and not simply copies of distorted or incomplete European originals.

Valignano's Embassy to Rome

Valignano's most daring plan was to send an embassy from the Christian daimyō of Japan to the pope. Valignano saw this as an opportunity to introduce Japanese culture to Europe and to press the needs of the Japanese mission. He also hoped that European civilization would impress the Japanese and thus make conversion easier. Valignano selected for his embassy four Christian young men—Mancio Itō, Michael Chijiwa, Julian Nakaura, and Martin Hara. These young men were not of common birth but closely connected to the daimyō they would represent. The four ambassadors, together with Valignano, sailed away from Nagasaki on 20 February 1582. Valignano had been in Japan for three years, and the embassy was to offer proof of both the past success and future hope of the Christian mission.

They were very well received throughout Europe and visited Pope Gregory XIII whose gifts they carried with them when they finally returned to Japan eight years after their departure. Julian, who with the other three had been admitted to the Jesuit order, was martyred for his faith at Nagasaki on 21 July 1633. It is said that he died whispering, " I am Julian Nakaura, who went to Rome."

A German newspaper reports the visit of the four Japanese Christian ambassadors to Pope Gregory XIII in Rome. In the center is the Jesuit Diego de Mesquita, who accompanied them.

PERSECUTION AND THE HIDDEN CHRISTIANS

The glorious company of the apostles,
the goodly fellowship of the prophets,
the noble army of martyrs,
the holy Church throughout the world.

"Te Deum Laudamus"

Change of Policy

Christianity is a religion that has experienced both successful mission and catastrophe. In the previous chapter, we saw the hope-filled process of the mission in Japan. Now we must turn to the agony, the story of how the solid start and valiant early success were completely and brutally suppressed. The persecution of Christianity in Japan stands as one of the worst persecutions that Christianity has had to endure in its long history.

What were the reasons for the change of policy? Why did the Japanese government begin to persecute Christians and eventually close the country to the outside world? Certainly, the country's political circumstances changed drastically from the open mood prevalent at the time of the arrival of the first Christian missionaries. Powerful new forces emerged to crush all that impeded the path to power. In the end, Christianity was destroyed not by the further disintegration of authority in Japan but by its ruthless reunification.

The demise of the Christian mission was the result of vital, individual personalities, just as its rise had been. Three military men, each of whom had made overtures to Christianity and each of whom became a powerful general, sought to control the destiny of Japan. Through their search for control, Oda Nobunaga (1534–82), Toyotomi Hideyoshi (1536–98), and Tokugawa Ieyasu (1542–1616) altered the fate of Christianity.

Oda Nobunaga

The daimyō of Owari, Oda Nobunaga, was the first to begin the process of national unification that would bring to an end the chaos and strife that characterized the age. He seemed to be indifferent to the beliefs of all organized religious groups, but to the extent that they threatened to interfere with his quest to power he could be ruthless, as he was with the armed Buddhist monks in the mountains around Kyoto. Frequently Nobunaga appeared friendly toward the Christian missionaries, perhaps because they were educated people, and he was deeply interested in European civilization. He received the Jesuit Luis Frois (1532–97) in April 1569, and we are indebted to Frois for his description of Nobunaga. He also met with Valignano in 1581 and encouraged Valignano's hopes for the Japanese mission. But this hope was quickly dashed. Only four months after Alessandro Valignano and the young Japanese ambassadors set sail for Europe, Oda Nobunaga met his end in a Kyoto temple through the treachery of one of his military generals, Akechi Mitsuhide.

Toyotomi Hideyoshi

Toyotomi Hideyoshi, a man of humble origins, was born in a small village in Nobunaga's domain. A military genius, Hideyoshi had advanced to become Nobunaga's chief general. He was campaigning for Nobunaga against the Mōri clan at the time of Nobunaga's death. Hideyoshi then abruptly withdrew from combat with the Mōri, returned to consolidate his own power, and continued with the task of unification. By 1590, his goal had been substantially achieved.

Hideyoshi initially continued a policy of toleration toward Christians and foreign traders. Like Nobunaga, he distrusted Buddhist power. He continued to reduce the power of Buddhist monks, building on Nobunaga's effective and merciless policy. In contrast, he was favorably disposed toward the Jesuit missionaries. He even went as far as giving a group of missionaries a personally guided tour of Osaka Castle. Valignano had always stressed, as had other Jesuit leaders before him, that it would be unwise and imprudent for missionaries to become involved in Japanese politics or to appear to take sides in domestic political conflicts. In 1586, Jesuit Superior Gaspar Coelho (1531–90) was received by Hideyoshi at his castle in Osaka. At this meeting, Valignano's caution began to seem a forewarning of disaster.

17. This bronze relief, created by the artist Funakoshi Yasutake, was dedicated on 10 June 1962 as a memorial to the twenty-six Catholics martyred in Nagasaki in 1597. With this martyrdom began more than forty years of brutal persecution of Catholics in

Japan. On his visit there in 1981, Pope John Paul II declared, "I hope that this monument will continue to talk to the world about love and about Christ." Among the twenty-six martyrs were six foreign and twenty Japanese Catholics.

PERSECUTION AND THE HIDDEN CHRISTIANS 43

It was Gaspar Coelho, selected to become Jesuit Superior of Japan by Valignano himself, who disregarded Valignano's warning when he met with Hideyoshi in Osaka. Hideyoshi mentioned to Coelho his future military ambitions, and Coelho not only offered Portuguese assistance, but also promised that he would martial the power of the Christian daimyō on Hideyoshi's behalf. Valignano later observed that Hideyoshi probably felt threatened by the idea of help from armed Christians, knowing full well that it could just as easily be mustered against him as for him. Hideyoshi continued his program of unification and successfully extended his military control to Kyushu. On 24 July 1587, while Hideyoshi and his army were resting at Hakata, Coelho traveled there to congratulate him. He arrived on a well-equipped ship, and Hideyoshi immediately requested to be taken on board. He inspected the ship and then asked to see the large Portuguese trading ship anchored in Hirado. The captain of the Portuguese *nao* explained to Hideyoshi that the ship could not be safely moved from Hirado to Hakata.

Hideyoshi seemed to accept the explanation the captain offered him, but less than twenty-four hours after this meeting, Hideyoshi lashed out against Christianity. It began as a short outburst against Takayama Ukon, a fervent Christian daimyō, with Hideyoshi demanding that he renounce his faith. When Takayama refused, Hideyoshi stripped him of his domain, issued an edict banishing the Jesuits from Japan, and took direct control of the port of Nagasaki. Reasons for his sudden outburst have been speculated to range from fear to an outpouring of drunken rage. Hideyoshi might have been goaded by his physician, Seiyakuin, who was an avowed enemy of Christianity, or Coelho's naive confidences could have spurred Hideyoshi's fear of Portuguese territorial ambitions. The actual cause of his anger remains unknown, and Hideyoshi's tirade, although violent while it lasted, subsided quickly. Hideyoshi did not pursue these policies; the missionaries did not leave, and no attempt was made to ensure that they leave.

During the next decade, Christian conversions continued and missionary effort took place against a backdrop of intermittent anger on the part of Hideyoshi. Although the edicts were not rescinded, they were not enforced. Coelho died in 1590 and was replaced by Pedro Gomez, who appears to have been a much more sensible man. Nagasaki, though under Hideyoshi's control, remained an active Catholic center.

Valignano came back to Japan with his young Christian ambassadors in July 1590. These four had been sumptuously received in Europe and were accorded a lavish, formal reception by Hideyoshi, who, following custom, exchanged gifts with Valignano. Valignano's presence—or rather his intelligence and diplomatic skills—helped ease the situation, and because Hideyoshi had formally received Valignano, the Christian community felt reassured that Hideyoshi's fury had little permanent significance. Yet, despite Valignano's visit, the edicts remained in force. Valignano was well aware these laws could be given substance in a moment and advocated caution within the Christian community. Again, Valignano's warning would appear, in retrospect, to have been a prophecy of the horror to come.

The situation worsened with the arrival in Japan of Franciscan missionaries. Rivalry emerged between the different missions, with the eager new missionaries lacking the circumspection that the Jesuits had struggled so long to learn. The Franciscans were new to the subtleties of Japanese politics, and they could not understand the Jesuit stance since the baptism of new converts continued in defiance of Hideyoshi's policies. On 19 October 1596, however, the reason for the Jesuits' caution became clear.

Nagasaki Martyrdom

On 19 October a Spanish ship named the *San Felipe* ran aground at the port of Urado in Shikoku. Hide-

Oda Nobunaga.

Toyotomi Hideyoshi.

yoshi ordered that the cargo be confiscated. The Spaniards, of course, protested. Hideyoshi then ordered a list to be made of all the Christians living in Kyoto.

On 8 December Hideyoshi initiated his first violent action against the Franciscans and their converts living in Kyoto and Osaka. Twenty-six were arrested and detained. They were sentenced to death on 31 December 1596. On 3 January each of the prisoners was mutilated and paraded through the city of Kyoto. Then, on 9 January, with one ear cut off and hands bound behind, they were forced to march south and west to Nagasaki—almost one full month in the bitter cold of winter. On 5 February 1597, they were publicly executed, speared to death while hanging on crosses set on a small hill overlooking the town. Martyred there were twenty Japanese, four Spaniards, one Indo-Portuguese, and one Mexican; three of the martyrs were young boys. This was only the beginning. Intermittent persecution followed and this eventually became systematic in the brutalities of the Tokugawa purge.

Tokugawa Ieyasu

In March 1597, Hideyoshi formally reiterated the ban against the Jesuits and further anti-Christian pressure was exerted. But on 16 September 1598, before his intentions became fully clear, Hideyoshi died, and Japan was once again plunged into a power struggle for political authority. Christians could only stand on the sidelines and wait.

From Hideyoshi's five strongest military leaders Tokugawa Ieyasu emerged victorious. In 1603 he was appointed shogun; this title signified the highest military authority and had eluded both Nobunaga and Hideyoshi. Ieyasu had moved the center of his activities to Edo in 1590, thereby establishing what was to be one of the world's largest seventeenth-century cities, now the modern city of Tokyo. Ieyasu secured the foundations for a system of social control that would maintain the stability of Japanese society until its collapse and the restoration of imperial control in 1868.

Various factors influenced Ieyasu's policies toward Christians in Japan. The differing views of the Protestant Englishman William Adams, who arrived in Japan in 1600, the Dutch traders, and the Spaniards and Portuguese were responsible for making European religious rivalries between Protestants and Catholics visible in Japan. One side planted suspicions against the other, and Ieyasu, no doubt, was never entirely sure what these Christians were planning. He also feared the intrusion of any authority, religious or political, that might challenge his own.

Toward an Edict of Persecution

From 1602 until 1614, sporadic persecution of Christians continued in Japan. A number of the Christian daimyō apostatized and made no effort to subdue local anti-Christian persecutions. While Christian conversions continued at a slowed pace, it was clear that the future was more uncertain than ever before.

On 27 January 1614, Tokugawa Ieyasu's anti-Christian policy was revealed with the promulgation of an edict forbidding the Christian religion in Japan and ordering the expulsion of all foreign missionaries from the country. The daimyō were instructed to send all foreign and all Japanese religious personnel to Nagasaki for deportation to Macao or Manila.

The Japanese people were commanded to return to traditional religious beliefs, and by the end of 1614 many church buildings had been destroyed. Only thirty-seven missionaries were able to slip through Ieyasu's net of surveillance and remain in Japan to face the next—and final—stage in the dismantling of Christianity in Japan.

Martyrdom and Apostasy

Ieyasu died in 1616. His son, Tokugawa Hidetada, pursued an increasingly cruel and harsh policy toward Christianity. Christian martyrs throughout Japan—both Japanese and foreign—embraced their faith at pain of death.

In 1619, three foreign missionaries were martyred for defying Tokugawa law. These were the first executions of foreign priests in Japan since the martyrdoms of 1597. In 1620 two missionaries who were trying to reenter Japan were tried by the governor of Nagasaki and the daimyō of Hirado. This complicated trial resulted in the execution of the two priests, the Japanese captain and crew of the ship on which they were discovered, and all the Christian prisoners held in the Nagasaki and Suzuta jails. In 1622, on the same,

Tokugawa Ieyasu.

18. The graves of a family of three Catholic Christians martyred in the persecutions of the seventeenth century were camouflaged to resemble a sacred Shinto area. This grove is in Nagasaki Prefecture in the town of Ikizuki. In the seventeenth century many Catholics were forced to conceal their faith. Over half of the population of Ikizuki was then Christian, and when they

reemerged in the Meiji period their hidden faith had gradually developed into a religious blend of Buddhism and Catholicism. Many of the "Hidden Catholics" in other areas again became members of the Catholic Church in the Meiji period, but those of Ikizuki preferred to worship according to their hybrid faith, and to this day remain separated from the Catholic church.

Bearing the inscription "Praised be the Blessed Sacrament," this banner was flown by the Christian rebels at Shimabara.

small hill overlooking Nagasaki, fifty-one martyrs died for the same faith as the twenty-six martyred there a generation before.

The number of martyrdoms increased. Hidetada's son, Iemitsu, intensified the persecution of Christians after succeeding to the position of shogun in 1623. He began his rule by presiding over a mass martyrdom where fifty Christians were burned at the stake. Iemitsu's persecution of Christians developed into an organized system of brutal torture aimed at effecting apostasy.

For several years, a few brave missionaries continued to work in disguise, harbored and protected by ordinary Japanese people. A bounty was offered for missionaries and for those who gave them assistance, and people suspected of Christian sympathies were forced to trample on religious pictures and insignia. The government continued implementing trade policies that would culminate in the almost total isolation of the country.

The Shimabara Rebellion

The closing incident of Christian persecution, the Shimabara rebellion, which began in late 1637, was a tragic, futile outburst. The missionary policy had always been one of passive resistance to the persecution raging through Japan. Unlike Buddhist groups which maintained armies, Christians had not been militant. In an impoverished village on the Shimabara peninsula of northwest Kyushu, the first and only Christian military stand took place. The incident began when a tax collector of the daimyō of Shimabara assaulted the daughter of a leading farmer. The farmer killed the tax collector, after which the entire village joined the insurrection. A majority, but not all, of the 37,000 insurrectionists were Christian. Those that were, displayed religious emblems and banners in defiance. After an attack on Shimabara Castle failed, the army of rebels took over the abandoned Hara Castle, which proved to be a remarkably strong fortress. The Christian army survived and came out ahead on several assaults, but by early April 1638, the defenders' position was desperate and on 12 April, a frontal assault finally got through their outer defenses. By 15 April, every rebel—every man, woman, and child—had been killed in battle or executed afterward.

By 1639, there were no members of the clergy active in Japan. The Tokugawa policy makers had forbidden all contact with the outside world, with the exception of severely limited and controlled trade with the Chinese and Dutch. The country was closed, seemingly forever.

Hidden Christians

During the early years of its persecution, the Catholic church managed to survive by two important devices. First was the *goningumi*, or groups of five households, that met together and kept the faith alive. Second, Japanese and European missionaries traveled about in disguise, usually at night, from one group to another, continuing their ministry. But with the final expulsion of foreign clergy and the success of the methods of capturing and executing any who again tried to enter the country, Christianity in Japan—as far as the Tokugawa government and the Christian headquarters in Europe were concerned—was dead. But amazingly, an underground church managed to survive by means of a complicated organizational system.

The Catholics who preserved their faith through this system are often called the *kakure*, or "hidden," Christians. The leader of a wide area was the elder (*chōkata*). He kept the records and the church calendar and communicated to the others the days of Christian festivals and events. In each small group (*kori*), there was the baptizer (*mizukata*), the catechist (*oshiekata*), and the listener (*kikikata*) who passed on local communications. The accuracy with which some of the Latin baptismal formulas were transmitted through this organization for over two hundred years enabled the Congregation of the Holy Office in Rome to declare them valid in 1865. Other matters became distorted with the passage of time. The central act of devotional life was the recitation of liturgical prayers (*orashio*) taught by the catechist and recited by the members. A great deal of syncretism took place, and when these Christians reemerged in the late nineteenth century, some of them did not rejoin the Catholic church but remained as an independent group (sometimes called *hanare*, or "separatist," Christians). They continue to exist in various isolated locations around Kyushu, retaining the same offices and operating mostly in secret. Debate exists as to whether or not they can be classified as Christian since they refuse to mingle with other Christian groups.

The Christian Legacy

Although the Christian believers seemed to vanish completely, the first Christians left a legacy which scholars claim continued to bear fruit in various ways. In social work, they left the tradition of caring for the poor and needy. This encouraged Buddhist institutions to do the same and thus enriched the ideal of social conscience in Japan. They stressed monogamous marriage and fidelity. They elevated the status of the common people. The educational importance of Christian culture was not lost, and the government continued to make use of important books written on scientific subjects by Jesuits. The influence of Barbarian scholarship (*Nambangaku*) and of Dutch learning (*Rangaku*), for example in the study of medicine, continued throughout the period. A further claim has been made that the monotheism of the Christian religion found its way into Japanese religious consciousness and is today expressed in Omotokyō and Tenrikyō, two of the so-called New Religions that draw heavily on Shinto beliefs.

After the Catholic Century came the Age of Silence. Not a public Christian sound was heard until after the arrival of Commodore Perry's flagship on Sunday, 18 June 1853. Japan wakened to the modern world and to Protestant Christianity at the same time.

João Rodrigues (1562–1633) arrived in Japan at the age of fifteen, and it was there that he became a member of the Jesuit Order. His command of the Japanese language was powerful, and he became the foremost Jesuit interpreter of both the Japanese language and culture. His masterwork, the *Arte da Lingoa de Iapam*, was the first systematic grammar of Japanese compiled in a Western language. Though dated in 1604, this comprehensive text was actually published in 1608. Rodrigues often served as the interpreter for both Hideyoshi and Tokugawa.

Artifacts remaining from the era of Catholic persecutions attest to the tenacity of the faith of Japanese Christians.

19. The Our Lady of the Rosary *fumie* is an example of the plaques that Japanese were forced to trample to prove they were not Christian. Those Christians who refused to tread on the sacred pictures were put to death. (*above left*)

20. This figure ostensibly depicts the Buddhist deity Kannon, whose female identity deftly provided concealment for the reverence of the Virgin Mary. Such statues of Kannon holding a child became known as the Maria-Kannon and were secretly revered by the "Hidden Christians" who continued in their Catholic faith. (*above*)

21. The Virgin Mary and other Catholic religious symbols were exquisitely carved and concealed within utensils such as those pictured here. (*left*)

22. Shimabara Castle in northwest Kyushu at sunset. Shimabara Castle, rebuilt in 1964, was originally built from stones transported from nearby Hara Castle. Hara Castle provided the almost unassailable fortress in which, in 1638, Christian-affiliated rebels, driven by poverty, held out against the oppressive daimyō of the Shimabara area. At the site of the ruins of Hara Castle remain only scattered stones and a cross dedicated to the more than 37,000 rebels who died there in a vain attempt to resist the poverty imposed by the tyranny of the Tokugawa government and its methods of social control. (*right*)

MEIJI-ERA CHRISTIAN MISSIONS

Let the world return to the ancient days of Bushido. Nay, I mean what I want to see is the baptized Bushido.

Uemura Masahisa

Japan Again Meets the Gospel

The curtain of seclusion that surrounded Japan during the period of Tokugawa rule was thrust aside when a squadron of "black ships" steamed into Uraga Bay in 1853. Commodore Matthew Perry, in command of the four gunboats, brought a message from American President Millard Fillmore, who had sent Perry to Japan "to demand as a right, and not to solicit as a favor, those acts of courtesy which are due from one civilized country to another." This important decision in American foreign policy helped propel Japan into the modern world.

When Perry arrived, there already were progressive elements in Japan seeking to improve the economic quality of life and, at the same time, move the country toward a much needed political modernization. Many daimyō knew that some kind of industrial development was necessary if Japan were to occupy a secure place within a rapidly modernizing world. The forces pushing Japan forward were coupled with a growing fear of the power of Western colonialism, for despite the policy of seclusion the Japanese were well aware of China's fate at the hands of the British. The alternatives to a trade agreement willingly entered into were clear to the Japanese, and they knew that the challenge offered by the arrival of the black ships was a technological one. Technologically the West had moved forward during the two centuries that Japan had stood still. These two forces, the desire for change and the fear of what refusal could bring, led to revolution and political modernization. The Meiji Restoration in 1868, named after the emperor who was its rallying point, marked the end of over 250 years of Tokugawa control and dismantled the shogunate administration with the reinstatement of direct imperial rule.

In 1854, Perry received Japan's answer to President Fillmore's letter. The Treaty of Kanagawa, which provided for the opening of two remote ports to refuel and resupply American ships, was immediately followed by further demands for trade. Then came the demand for access to a far more precious resource: the souls of the Japanese people. Once again missionaries pressed to follow in the wake of merchant traders.

Thanks to the growing enthusiasm for religious evangelism in the United States, money began to be collected for a Japan mission twenty-five years before Commodore Perry received his commission to go to Japan, and by the time American mission work finally did begin, over $4,000 had been raised. American Christians made missionary work in Japan a special concern and exerted the strongest influence on what has been called Japan's "Protestant Century."

In 1856, Townsend Harris became the first American consul to Japan. Because of his skillful negotiations to ensure their religious freedom, foreigners were once again permitted restricted residence in Japan and were allowed to worship freely and bring books into Japan as they pleased. While Christianity still remained prohibited for the Japanese, the banned religion was once again an active force, if only through the strength of its adherents' personalities and the influence of their books.

Entering on the strength of the trade treaties, Catholic, Protestant, and Orthodox missionaries all arrived in Japan at about the same time. They came in 1859, ostensibly to minister to the religious needs of the foreign community, and they settled in Yokohama, Nagasaki, and elsewhere. American representatives of the Episcopal church, the Presbyterian church, and the Dutch Reformed church were among the first Protestants in the field. The first modern missionaries included not only ministers, but doctors like J. C. Hepburn. Dr. Hepburn opened a clinic and, in addition, produced many works on the Japanese language as part of his missionary devotion.

The missionaries' early years were difficult while the edict against Japanese conversion was still in force. It was not until 1873 that, under international pressure, the proscription was removed from public noticeboards. This moved the Reverend Guido Verbeck of the Dutch Reformed church to declare that a second phase in Protestant missions had begun, and that the period of "progressive realization and performance" could finally build on the preceding period of "preparation and promise."

The Reemergence of the Hidden Christians

On 17 March 1865, the first Japanese group of Hidden Christians revealed themselves in Nagasaki at a newly built church: the underground Catholic church had surfaced.

Caution was initially required since the anti-Christian laws were still in force at the time. Indeed, it was not long before official suspicion was roused, and it then became clear that dangers still existed for Japanese Christians. Danger notwithstanding, about twenty thousand Hidden Christians came forward between the years 1865 and 1867. They were encouraged by missionaries to defy government ordinances and worship openly, but from mid-1867 persecution of Japanese Catholics began again and during 1869, sixty died in prison and over three thousand were exiled.

It was just at this time that the Tokugawa shogunate collapsed and the Emperor Meiji assumed authority over the government of Japan. To develop an informed relationship with the modern world, the new government, in 1871, commissioned a group (the Iwakura Mission) to travel to Europe and America to study and learn from foreign customs. When word reached Europe that persecution of Catholics in Japan had begun again, international public outrage exerted enormous pressure on this mission and almost defeated its purpose. The stern warning from world opinion forced the government to reverse its policy and withdraw the proscription against Christianity, and it was removed from public noticeboards on 19 February 1873. The conditions surrounding the repeal of the proscription are a good example of what one Japanese scholar has said is characteristic of Japanese society —that the force for major social and political change comes invariably from outside Japan. The converse is also noted: once started, movements within Japanese society often are stopped only by pressure from the outside.

The women assembled in this picture for Sunday School service were among the first Japanese women to hear the Protestant Christian message. This photo dates from the early Meiji period and probably depicts a Bible study lesson on a Christmas theme.

MEIJI-ERA CHRISTIAN MISSIONS 53

24. The seclusion of Japan was brought to an end by the appearance in Uraga Bay of a squadron of black steamships under the command of the American Commodore M. Perry. In the wake of the ships came trade treaties and missionaries.

23. This brightly colored Japanese woodblock print humorously depicts the cultural confusion that surrounded Japan's reencounter with the West after more than 200 years of self-imposed seclusion. Many differences are recorded here, and the most obvious ones leap immediately to the eye. In the upper right-hand corner rides a Western horseman carrying a barber pole. Beside him is a donkey carrying a Bible; nearby are a Western-style chair and a boot. In the extreme upper left-hand corner rides a Japanese horseman with bow and arrow. Beside him, the *Four Chinese Classics*. Flying in front of both riders are their respective flags. Sailing on the ocean are a Western paddle-wheel steamboat and a Japanese sailboat. In the middle right-hand section of the print, a battle is waging between a Western oil lamp and a Japanese oil lamp assisted by a Japanese paper lantern. According to the Japanese description, the Western-style lamp is vanquishing the Japanese lamps because of its ability to shine brighter. In the right-hand foreground, a Japanese bird of prey holding a Japanese umbrella is jostling a Western bird of prey wielding a Western-style umbrella. Half hidden in the middle of the print is a steam engine, transportation without rival in Japan in this period. In front of the steam engine, a Western postbox is handily defeating its Japanese equivalent which collects and transports the mail on foot, wandering through the streets of Japanese cities. In the front left-hand corner it appears as if Japanese woodblock prints are going to defeat photographs, but the palanquin bearers behind—at two to a palanquin—are being routed by the one-man rikisha. Take another, closer look, for the comparisons are endless and endlessly fascinating.

25. The missionaries pictured here were among the first representatives of the American Congregational church sent to Japan. Standing on the right is Otis Cary, and seated before him is his wife, Ellen. The name of the woman sitting at Ellen Cary's feet is uncertain, but she is presumed to be a Miss Wilson. In the center, standing and seated, are Dr. and Mrs. Berry, and on the left are Belle (standing) and James Pettee, cousins of the Carys and fellows in missionary work. This picture was taken in Okayama in the 1880s, shortly after this missionary group had taken up their work there. They were the first Westerners ever to live in Okayama. The citizens of Okayama gathered in amazement as Governor Takasaki, in full formal dress complete with stovepipe hat, insisted on rowing the missionaries around the lake in Kōrakuen every Sunday in a rowboat he had purposely brought from Kobe for the enlightenment and Westernization of the Okayama populace. Mr. Cary's two-volume *A History of Christianity in Japan* is still the most detailed account in English on this subject.

Japanese Reembrace Christianity

Many books have been written which recount in detail the names of individual missionaries and the groups they represented. What is of interest to us here is the dynamism behind the spread of Protestant Christianity in Meiji Japan.

Conversion to Protestant Christianity took three main forms. One was spontaneous, as is illustrated by the case of Murata Wakasa. Murata was a Tokugawa official and scholar who, in 1855, found a copy of the New Testament in Dutch floating in Nagasaki harbor. At the time it was still illegal to show even an interest in Christianity, but he and his brother studied the Bible together for several years in secret. Finally they sought out Guido Verbeck of the Dutch Reformed church, who had arrived in Nagasaki in 1859. Murata then began an indirect Christian tutorship with Verbeck using his brother and his cousin as go-betweens. For three years Verbeck participated in this strange question-and-answer dialogue until finally, in 1866, Murata Wakasa arrived in person with his brother, two sons, and sixty retainers, all seeking Christian baptism. He was baptized on the Day of Pentecost in 1866 and became Japan's first Protestant convert.

Another powerful means of Christian evangelism was through the personal influence of non-missionary, Christian teachers and the youthful bands that were their students. The traditional values held by these Japanese students blended well with the stoicism of their military teachers. The third form of diffusion was through the dedicated effort and enthusiasm of Japanese Christian individuals who, after receiving the gospel, sought to further the spread of the Christian faith. Many of these influential individuals learned of the Christian message while a member in one of the Meiji Christian bands, others through personal quest.

Niijima Jō

What sort of Japanese were becoming Christians? The story of Niijima Jō (1843–90) is often considered as representative. It begins with the dreams of a young scholar-samurai who came from the village of Annaka in what is now Gumma Prefecture. Niijima was an elite member of his community, a samurai brought up in the household of the daimyō. His grandfather was the daimyō's steward, and his father was the domain's calligraphy master. When he was about twenty, he chanced upon a Chinese translation of an English summary of the Bible and became interested in Christianity. Niijima at that time had deep longings for his future and for the greatness of his nation, but he chafed at the rigid demand of unquestioned loyalty to the shogunate. In other words, like many of those who came after him, in his soul Christianity and patriotism combined. He was deeply attracted by the civilization that produced the great ships, and he was fascinated with the science of the Dutch, British, and Americans. He decided to leave Japan and search for wider horizons abroad.

In spite of the death penalty still imposed on anyone who tried to leave the country, Niijima set off for Hokkaido to seek a route to leave Japan. In Hakodate he taught Japanese to a Russian priest while learning English from a shipping clerk. In 1864, the shipping clerk helped him to board an American ship as a stowaway. He sold both his samurai swords: for the long one he got his passage to America, for the short one he was able to buy a Chinese version of the New Testament. Niijima was befriended on his way to America, entered Amherst College in 1867, and went on to study at Andover Theological Seminary. He served briefly as an interpreter for the Iwakura Mission of 1871 when it was in the United States and subsequently received permission to return to Japan. He continued to work at his studies and was ordained a Congregational minister. In 1875 he returned to Japan, eager to bring to fruition his dream of founding a Christian college in his own country.

When he returned to Annaka he found many of his close relatives ill and his once-wealthy family almost penniless. He spent some time in his home village, introducing his faith and starting up a Bible reading group among the samurai he had left over ten years before. This would prove to be the impetus for the development of the Protestant church in the Annaka region. Niijima continued on to Kyoto, where he founded the Christian college Dōshisha, which is today one of Japan's leading private institutions of higher education.

The history of Niijima Jō illustrates two important points. It reveals the dissatisfaction of typical samurai

Niijima Jō.

with the premodern status quo, and it indicates how Christianity spread through influential members of the samurai class as a result of the personal dynamism of new samurai converts. Samurai like Niijima Jō who converted to Christianity often became the bulwark of the emerging church and brought to the church prevailing samurai values.

The Christian Bands

The Sapporo Band of Christians gathered under the tutelage of William S. Clark, who is still remembered today for exhorting, "Boys be ambitious for Christ." Clark was president of the Massachusetts Agricultural College. He went to Hokkaido in 1876 in response to a Japanese government request that he help establish an agricultural college in Sapporo. The fifty-year-old American Civil War veteran stayed less than one year in the Hokkaido area, but within that year every one of his fifteen students requested Christian baptism. After Clark had left, these zealous students went on to convince the class of the following year to sign Clark's "Covenant of Believers in Jesus."

Clark received reluctant permission to teach ethics and he used the Bible as his textbook. In this way he combined evangelism with teaching. From the Sapporo Band came many great names in Japanese history, including Nitobe Inazō, who became under-secretary general to the League of Nations, and Uchimura Kanzō, founder of the non-church movement.

The second band which influenced the modern Japanese Christian community was established in Kumamoto. Captain L. L. Janes, a graduate of West Point and also an American Civil War officer, was invited in 1871 by the daimyō of the area, who wanted to set up a school in the castle town of Kumamoto. Although the purpose of the school was not religious, after five years of careful and discreet work Janes was able to indirectly include religious education as part of the training. Because of Janes's character and his military approach to the young men, he influenced about forty of his students to join him in a pilgrimage to the top of Mt. Hanaoka near Kumamoto on 30 January 1876. There they pledged their loyalty to Jesus Christ as emancipator of the Japanese nation.

Once news of their conversion got out, a great deal of pressure was brought to bear on these young men and against Janes. The authorities did not renew Janes's contract and the school was closed. Before Janes left Japan, he introduced the young men to Niijima Jō, who had just established Dōshisha, and members of the Kumamoto Band went to join him in Kyoto and study there. Numerous future leaders of the Japanese Christian community were part of this group: Kozaki Hiromichi, later to become President of Dōshisha, Ebina Danjō, one of Japan's finest theologians, and Kanamori Tsūrin, perhaps the most famous evangelist of his day, were all offshoots of the Kumamoto Band.

The third band to influence the beginnings of Meiji-period Christianity was the Yokohama Band, which flourished under the inspired direction of Dr. Samuel R. Brown of the Dutch Reformed Church in America. It grew out of a school for boys conducted in the homes of missionaries where English and other general subjects were taught. The teachers at this informal school included Brown, as well as other well-known men such as Dr. Hepburn and the Reverend J. H. Ballagh. It was under Ballagh's inspiration that the first Protestant congregation of modern Japan came into being.

Japan's First Protestant Church

In January 1872, the missionaries and some of the English-speaking residents of Yokohama united to observe an annual week of prayer under the auspices of the World Evangelical Alliance. A few young Japanese attended these meetings and were inspired by their fervor. After the week had finished, some of these young Japanese continued to meet with Ballagh for prayer and study. Ballagh taught them from the Book of Acts.

This study group produced remarkable results: nine young men requested baptism. Up until then, only ten Japanese had been baptized. The rich devotional temperament of these Japanese deeply touched the foreign observers. Two middle-aged men who had previously been baptized, Mr. Ogawa (who became the church's first elder) and Mr. Nimura (who became its first deacon), joined these nine boys, and under the leadership of Ballagh they formed Japan's first Protestant church on 10 March 1872, the Nihon Kirisuto Kōkai, the Church of Christ in Japan. The goal was to establish a church that would become a national church of Japan, one not allied to any particular Western denomination. That ideal would prove to be very hard to realize.

Early Japanese Christian converts brought their traditional values and future hopes with them when they became Christian. Some of Japan's traditional values, especially those of the samurai, blended well with the nineteenth-century Puritan aspects of Protestant Christianity. Many Meiji-period Japanese saw the economic and political institutions of their youth torn down before their eyes. In a time of such rapid and far-reaching change, Christianity offered a refuge. By the time there was no longer a need for such a refuge, however, many Japanese Christian converts had already transplanted their original values into the receptive soil of the Christian church.

26. The lovely red-brick chapel on the Dōshisha University campus attracts many visitors. Designed by D. C. Greene in 1886, the chapel was designated an Important Cultural Property in 1963 and was included in a series of Commemorative Issue Stamps depicting outstanding examples of Western architecture from the Meiji period.

27. Annaka Church, the place of worship of Japan's oldest Protestant congregation, dates back to 1875 and is the result of the mission work of Niijima Jō. Before establishing Japan's first Protestant College, Dōshisha University in Kyoto, Niijima made a pilgrimage to his home town to share the Protestant message with his family and friends. He had left home some years before, risking his life and his future, to go to America to study the Protestant Christian faith. The Annaka Church is in Gumma Prefecture, about three hours northwest of Tokyo, and is a classic example of Protestant simplicity. On the left wall of the chapel hangs a portrait of Niijima.

28. The Ōura Catholic Church, first established in about 1568, is the oldest Christian church in Japan. The Gothic-style building pictured here was designed by Father Frue in 1863 and was built by Koyama Hidenoshi; construction was finished in December 1864. This was the place of worship of the twenty-six Nagasaki martyrs (martyred in 1597), and it was to the priest of this church that the first of the "Hidden Christians" revealed themselves in the early Meiji period. They came forward on 17 March 1865 declaring to the startled amazement of all, "We are of the same faith." Ōura Church was designated a National Treasure on 23 January 1933.

58 CHRISTIANITY AND JAPAN

CHARIOTS OF FIRE

O God, make me like Christ.

Kagawa Toyohiko

Japanese Christian Leadership

The emergence of a strong Japanese leadership within the Christian church became possible after the early Meiji-period hostility to Christianity subsided. The average Japanese of the mid-1880s harbored considerable suspicion towards the faith, not from any basis in informed criticism, but from the Tokugawa-period image of Christianity as an alien religion that threatened Japanese culture. Christianity gradually came to be associated with progress and the mood in Japan towards this foreign religion became more positive. In 1884, Fukuzawa Yukichi, the founder of Japan's prestigious Keio University and one of the leading Meiji intellectuals, commended Christianity because of its wealth, its virtue, and its ability to attract "persons of rank." In this changed atmosphere, four types of pivotal Christian personalities emerged that have given the Christian church in Japan much of its definitive and lasting character.

Intellectuals

By far the most predominant type of Christian personality in Japan is the intellectual. This accounts for the high value placed on education by Japanese Christians. Japanese Christians have been active in all academic fields, and in theology, several original Japanese thinkers have emerged. Uemura Masahisa, founder of a new Reformed tradition, was a man of outstanding intellect whom we shall discuss in the following chapter. In addition, Ebina Danjō and Uchimura Kanzō deserve our special attention here.

One of the foremost thinkers of the early period of Protestant evangelism was Ebina Danjō (1856–1939), whose life work covered ministries in Gumma, Kumamoto, Kobe, and Tokyo. He succeeded to the chancellorship of Dōshisha after Niijima. His independence of thought was revealed in a famous controversial exchange with Uemura Masahisa, which was conducted at length in the pages of the two Christian journals they edited.

Ebina's views blended the influence of German liberalism with a desire to make Christianity intelligible (but not necessarily acceptable) to Japanese people who saw no connection between belief in the Christian faith and the social, scientific, and cultural developments of the West. Ebina did see such a connection, and to this modern presentation of the doctrines of the church Uemura reacted as a stern orthodox Calvinist condemning heresy. Ebina's thought, which Uemura condemned, combined three elements. Ebina's strict upbringing in Confucian ethics resulted in his belief in a natural and rational type of religious revelation. He viewed revelation as derived from the idea of fundamental human moral sense. He stressed that this moral sense was the basis for the reconciliation between Christianity and other religious belief systems. He insisted that humanity had an inherently good conscience. In this way, he retained a deep sense of the natural good in Japanese Shinto thought and tried to enrich and develop it. He never rejected his early ethical training and sought in Christianity the confirmation of all that had been worthwhile in it.

The second characteristic of Ebina's thought came from the prevailing currents of Meiji liberal intellectualism. He was twelve years old when the Meiji Restoration took place and he was forty before the reaction against Western influence began. In his writings, his desire to be Japanese and yet to rise above nationalism is clear. Ebina sought ecumenicity and universality, and he sought a way to express Christianity that was free of any attachment to sterile Greek metaphysical categories. He wanted a form of expression that took into full account social and scientific developments.

The third characteristic was Ebina's use of his own religious experience as a basis from which to formulate theological concepts. While he sometimes spoke mystically, there was always a sense that he had transposed the high ethics of Confucianism to the higher ones of Christ. Sin, forgiveness, and atonement were not his central concerns. He struggled to give expression to a Christianity that would encompass a rapprochement with Buddhism—a Christianity that was enriched by the depth of Oriental religion. This would enable Christianity to fulfill its potential in the world. Christianity, for Ebina, provided the ultimate moral inspiration. Christ's approachability made closeness with God possible. In Ebina's theology, Christ became the Universal Person who first experienced what all men who lose preoccupation with the self may experience with God.

> Christ's death was not a legal ransom or any theory of this kind. It was his willing self-sacrifice for the building of the Kingdom. It was his witness to God of man's love and his witness to man of God's love. His death is entrance to eternal life. To die with him and to live with him is to understand death.

Such sentiments may not bring joy to orthodox ears, yet Ebina's words clearly demonstrate the struggle of a first-generation Japanese Christian with the meaning of faith in Jesus Christ.

Ebina's theological tradition is best represented in modern times by Kitamori Kazō and his theology of the Pain of God. Like Ebina, Kitamori tried to introduce a new framework of thought for the understanding of the gospel. He also grappled with the problems of indigenization and Christian evangelism.

As nineteenth-century Protestant Japanese Christians developed their theological understanding, they also radicalized the church. The most radical theology to come out of this era was that of a young man who attended the Sapporo Agricultural College where William Clark had taught. At first this young man vowed that he would declare war on Christianity, on the Christians, and on the Christian God. He perceived Christianity to be an evil which must not be permitted to take root in Japan. But like St. Paul, his resistance led him toward what he undertook to challenge: Uchimura Kanzō (1861–1930) came to embrace Christianity and found that he did not cease to be Japanese.

Uchimura went to America in 1884 and worked in a hospital for retarded children. One evening, while serving his turn on the night shift, he felt the sense of religious calling that is often described in the Bible by Old Testament prophets. That evening, he penned in the flyleaf of his Bible the words of the new vow that he had made. This vow would shape the rest of his life. "I for Japan, Japan for the world, the world for Christ, and all for God."

Uchimura went on to Amherst College in 1887. When he returned to Japan he became a history teacher at a Tokyo high school. In 1891 he refused to bow in reverence before the scroll that contained the emperor's edict on the purpose of education. This show of independence led to a storm of controversy that left Uchimura unemployed and nursing a bout of pneumonia. After filling various other posts, he devoted himself entirely to writing. His newspaper articles deeply touched the conscience of Japanese society. In 1901 he formed a new group and established the non-church movement (mukyōkai).

The non-church movement developed out of his practice of giving lectures and charging an attendance fee. He had no ritual, no ceremony, no organization, and no sacraments, for he wanted to free Japanese Christianity from Western influence. Uchimura simply adhered to scripture and to the meaning of the Cross of Christ; his style combined the simplicity of primitive Christianity with the traditional Japanese ideal of the teacher (sensei). Uchimura believed that society could be reformed through the reform of the individual. He also believed that Christ had not intended to found a church, and since no church could possibly be pure, he felt it was better to abandon churches and deny any idea of historical continuity within them. When he founded the non-church movement, Uchimura confirmed that for him the risen Christ is beyond history.

Describing his conception of the true church, Uchimura wrote:

> Its roof is the blue sky, its rafters are the stars, its floor is the green fields and the colorful flowers, its musical instruments are the branches of pine trees and its musicians are the little birds of the forest; its pulpit is the summit of the mountain and the preacher is God.

The Social Gospel

The second type of Japanese Christian personality placed action before intellect, love before faith. Principal among these were Christian philanthropists and social workers like Yamamuro Gumpei and Kagawa Toyohiko.

Kagawa Toyohiko (1888–1960) was born in Kobe on 10 July. He was the son of a wealthy and influential man, and his father was secretary to the Emperor Meiji's Privy Council. Since Kagawa's mother was not his father's legal wife, his position was a difficult one, and when his father died Kagawa could make no strong claim to the family's fortune. Kagawa first became influenced by Christianity while he was in high school. At that time, he met a Christian teacher and was introduced to two missionaries; when he became a Christian his family disowned him. On his own, he was able to put himself through Meiji Gakuin University, a college with Presbyterian connections, and he studied to become a minister. During the course of his studies, his faith deepened into one of intense social concern with a passion for action. He often prayed, "O God, make me like Christ." His effort to achieve this prayer is evident in his life's work.

Kagawa worked from 1909 to 1914 in the Kobe slum area of Shinkawa. There he put his principles of Christian love into practice. Feeling the need of further education, he went to America to attend Princeton in 1914. He completed degrees at both the university and the theological seminary. Kagawa wrote *Shisen o koete* (Crossing the Death Line) in 1920, and this book had an enormous impact on stimulating the social conscience of the Japanese people. Kagawa advocated that the Japanese people revere laborers in order to counteract the undue respect in which ancient heroes were held. He claimed that those heroes were nothing more than brigands. Kagawa wished all people equally to have life, liberty, and autonomy, but he believed in non-violent change. As a Christian Socialist he taught a religiousness based on guild socialism; the British Labour party was his ideal. And he believed that the Christian God spoke directly to the conscience of each human being—Christian and non-Christian.

Out of recognition for his achievements, the Japanese government started a ten-million-dollar anti-slum drive. He was also made one of the 180 members of a special commission to oversee rebuilding after the earthquake of 1 September 1923 that virtually destroyed the Tokyo area. Kagawa's non-violence predated that of Gandhi: Kagawa actually criticized Gandhi for advocating narrow nationalism. His most famous book, *The Religion of Jesus*, came out in English in 1931. The message contained within this book is best summarized in Kagawa's own words: "We must love people before we argue with them. In that loving, God Himself will be revealed."

After World War II, Kagawa refused appeals that he become a politician and remained true to his ideal: he was a preacher until his death in 1960. He was always a versatile and creative man for all seasons.

Christian Feminism

The history of Christianity in Japan is incomplete without reference to the women who participated in Christian leadership and what they, in turn, achieved for women in Japan. There were many Japanese women in the forefront of the Christian movement. Tsuda Umeko, who pioneered higher education for women, and Kawai Michi, who was president of the Japan YWCA, are among the most outstanding.

Tsuda Umeko (1864–1929) was born in Tokyo, and was the daughter of Tsuda Sen, official English interpreter to the Tokugawa shogunate. The youngest of the five female members of the Iwakura Mission, Tsuda was sent to America in 1871 when she was only seven years old, and she stayed with the Charles Lanman family of Washington, D. C. They were a childless couple and treated her as if she were a favorite daughter. She asked to be baptized a Christian when she was nine years old. She received her primary and secondary education in Washington schools, but occasionally spent her summers with the religiously active Leonard Bacon family of Connecticut, who influenced Tsuda's commitment to education as a means of social reform.

She returned to Japan in 1882 at the age of 18 and was employed by the Imperial Household Department as an interpreter. In 1885, when the Peeresses' School was founded to educate the daughters of Japanese nobility, Tsuda became a teacher there. In 1889, she was allowed to keep her position and take a leave of absence to return to America to further her education. She entered Bryn Mawr College, in Philadelphia, where she studied biology and became an outstanding student. She graduated from Bryn Mawr in 1892, foregoing a career as a scientist, and returned to Japan in 1892 to resume teaching at the Peeresses' School.

In 1900, with money she had collected through donations from Philadelphia women for scholarships for Japanese women by giving lectures in America on Japan, Tsuda established a college, the Joshi Eigaku Juku (Women's School of English Studies; now Tsuda Juku Daigaku). Her goal was to provide higher education for Japanese women that would train them to be teachers of English. Joshi Eigaku Juku was the first professional school for women in Japan and among the first institutions for female higher education, opening one year after Nihon Joshi Daigaku (Japan Women's College). Tsuda conceived of her school as a non-sectarian Christian school. In 1904, Tsuda's school received government recognition as a professional school, and in 1905 Tsuda graduates were permitted to receive governmental teaching licenses without taking the regular governmental examination.

Tsuda was a committed feminist, concerned for the status of Japanese women. She saw traditional Japanese education as training women to be docile and obedient, and she wanted to encourage Japanese women to use their intelligence and develop self-confidence. She felt, however, that these qualities needed to be developed in a Christian environment. A Christian from the age of nine, and educated at Bryn Mawr, which had a Quaker background, Tsuda said the following, which expresses her educational philosophy:

Yet to encourage these [qualities], as some would do, without the basis of religion and specially Christianity, and without the development of mind and the reasoning powers, brings in the greatest elements of danger. What is needed is the growth of the spiritual life, a real training of the understanding, moral teachings that fit the new conditions of life in modern Japan, and which would develop a realization of the possibilities that come with freedom—in a word, Christian education on higher lines.

Tsuda believed that Christian education promoted spiritual growth and that Christian influence could improve the status of Japanese women. She was also an active writer and lecturer. She published the *Eibun Shimpō*, an English-language newspaper aimed at encouraging the spread of English in Japan. She toured America and Europe in 1907 and went again to America for the International Christian Student Conference in 1913. Until her death, she remained committed to both educational and Christian concerns.

Kawai Michi (1877–1953) was born in Mie Prefecture on the east coast of Japan. Her father's family had been Shinto priests for generations, but her father converted to Christianity and encouraged her to have a Christian primary education. She was educated at Hokusen Jogakkō, a girls' school in Sapporo, where she came under the influence of an American Christian teacher and became a Christian. Like Tsuda, she, too, went to Bryn Mawr College, and after her graduation, she returned to Japan in 1904 and became a teacher at Tsuda's school.

Kawai was one of Japan's prominent Christian workers and became General Secretary of Japan's Young Women's Christian Association (YWCA). Under her direction, the YWCA in Japan became an active center for reform. In 1929, she founded the Keisen Jogakuen ("Fountain of Blessings" School), which provided a Christian education for young women. She was a member of the Church of Christ and, as an active author and lecturer, stressed the importance of the Christian church in improving women's lives and of Christian education in improving women's minds.

Bridge Builders

The fourth type of Japanese Christian personality that emerged in the early Protestant period and is still very much a part of today's Japanese Christian community is best exemplified by Nitobe Inazō (1862–1933). Nitobe is not usually linked with Meiji-period Christians in quite the same way as Ebina and Uchimura are. His contribution to Japanese liberal thinking emerged from his Christianity (he was a member of the Sapporo Band), and his disciples have gone on to make a major contribution to liberal thought. Nitobe was one of the first Japanese to try to realize the ideal of being a bridge between Japan and the West. In his famous work *Bushido: The Soul of Japan*, he tried to explain the basic principles of Japanese culture to the modern world. Nitobe's thought most explicitly reveals the way Christianity could be linked with *bushidō*, the stoic samurai ethic of loyalty, perseverance, and avoidance of shame.

Nitobe's international ideal included his marriage to the Philadelphia Quaker, Mary Elkington. He was the first president of Japan Women's Christian College

Tsuda Umeko, the youngest of the women to participate in the 1871 Iwakura Mission, was seven years old when the left photo was taken prior to their departure. Umeko is seated second from the right. In the next photo, the same group is pictured in the new Western-style clothes they received after their arrival in America. Umeko is again second from the right.

Pictured here are the Japanese Christian ministers who assembled for a leadership conference held in Tokyo in May 1883. Seated in the front row, from left to right, are Nakajima Torajirō, Okuno Masatsuna, Matsuyama Takayoshi, Tsuda Sen, Ri Jutei, Yuasa Jirō, Kurimura Saehachi, and Ebina Danjō. Second row, from left to right: Morita Tahei, Hiraiwa Hiroyasu, Makioka Tetsuya, Tsuji Iruo, Uchimura Kanzō, Niijima Jō, Kimura Kumaji, Terasawa Hisakichi, and Ishihara Yasutarō. Third row: Ogimi Motoichirō, Katō Yūjirō, Ibuka Kajinosuke, Aoyama Junjirō, Miyagawa Tsuneteru, Yokoi Tokio, Inagaki Shin, and Koide Ichinosuke. Fourth row: Itō Tōkichi, Nagasaka Tsuyoshi, Hattori Ayao, Kozaki Hiromichi, Uemura Masahisa, Kanamori Tsūrin, Oshikawa Masayoshi, Wada Hidetoyo, and Uehara Hōryu. Last row: Asakawa Hiromi, Miura Tōru, Yoshioka Kōki, Kumano Yūshichi, Minagaki Shūgo, and a representative of a Bible sales company. Many of these men are still remembered today. Most notable among them are Tsuda Sen, father of Umeko; Ebina Danjō, early Meiji Christian intellectual; Uchimura Kanzō, founder of the non-church movement; Niijima Jō, founder of Dōshisha College; Kozaki Hiromichi, one of the presidents of Dōshisha; Uemura Masahisa, the dominant Japanese personality within the Presbyterian church.

and later became under-secretary to the League of Nations. He struggled valiantly through the collapse of the League of Nations after Japan's withdrawal from it, and he had to face danger in Japan as Japanese militarism began to take hold. He tried to give Japan the international scope and understanding which he thought it lacked. One can only speculate about what might have happened to Nitobe had he lived into the war years.

Nitobe's life and work remind us of one important contribution that Christianity has made to Japan— Christianity, and the work of Japanese Christians such as Nitobe, has helped Japan to be more a part of the rest of the modern world. Time and again, the forces for improvement, liberalization, and international awareness in Japan have been Christian forces. These have had, and are still having, a great progressive influence on modern Japanese society. As the end of the twentieth century approaches, the contributions of a Christian personality like Nitobe may prove to be the most important contributions—for Christianity, for Japan, and for us all.

MAINSTREAM CHURCHES

It is my confident belief that if the missionary societies are faithful to their charge up to the end of this century, you need not, after 1890, send any more missionaries to Japan.

Guido Verbeck in 1889

The Christian endeavor that swept nineteenth-century Japan followed a nondenominational pattern of religious inspiration. After the repeal of the prohibition of Christianity, the missionaries of the various denominations settled into the work of building a mission. These mainstream churches established a foundation for Christianity in Japan which still continues.

In the early days many hoped that a non-denominational, truly indigenous church could be established in Japan. Efforts to keep Japanese Christianity simple and direct failed. All the major Western denominations became individually entrenched, and today 150 Christian denominations are still represented in Japan. Of these, several have exerted a striking influence on the development of Japanese Christianity and are, therefore, considered part of the Christian mainstream. From within these denominations emerged the first Japanese Christian leaders.

Presbyterian and Dutch Reformed Churches

Among the first missionaries to Japan, those sent by the American missionary boards of the Dutch Reformed and Presbyterian churches of the United States were devoted, talented men who quickly assumed a position of leadership. Dr. Samuel R. Brown, an American sent by the Dutch Reformed church, greatly influenced Uemura Masahisa (1858–1925).

Uemura, the youngest member of the Yokohama Band, was baptized at the age of sixteen. He entered a theological seminary and went on to establish a preaching center (*dendōsho*), which was the first center for evangelism started by a Japanese. He founded his own Presbyterian congregation which struggled from the beginning to be an independently funded Japanese church.

In 1900, almost all the Protestant congregations relied on contributions from overseas. Uemura believed that such reliance delayed the development of a strong Japanese Christianity, for along with these donations inevitably came direction and influence.

Uemura decided to accept a life of poverty in order to establish a truly Japanese Christian church. Uemura's theology also encompassed a strong commitment to women's rights. The Presbyterian church in Japan was the first to ordain women, and among the first women ordained in Japan was Uemura's daughter, Tamaki.

The Congregational Church

The first representatives of the Congregational church were sent to Japan in 1869, ten years after the first American missionaries. Although Congregational missionary representation was delayed, the Congregationalist minister Niijima Jō and the educational institution he founded in 1875, Dōshisha, advanced Congregational church mission work.

The Congregational church, called the Kumiai Kyōkai in Japanese, became the largest Protestant denomination in the Meiji period. It had the most missionaries in the field, including, proportionately, the greatest number of female missionaries. There are many reasons for the church's rapid growth. The fact that the Congregational missionaries stressed education, as Niijima did, is an important one, for the avenues to all types of education were at that time in Japan severely restricted. Also, the Congregational mission (as well as the Presbyterian mission) was committed to promoting Japanese leadership, and in the struggle over local autonomy for Japanese churches, the Congregationalist's flexible and liberal policy toward religious independence proved very important. Among the strong Japanese Congregationalist leadership were members of the Kumamoto Band who had gone to Dōshisha to continue their education.

The Anglican-Episcopal Church

C. M. Williams arrived in Japan in 1859 as an American missionary for the Protestant Episcopal church. In 1887, the Anglican church and the American Episcopal church missions established the Nippon Seikōkai (the Holy Catholic Church of Japan).

29. Nicolai Cathedral, named for Father Nicolai who first shared the Orthodox religion with the Japanese people, was severely damaged in the bombing of Tokyo during World War II. The church pictured here was rebuilt after the war.

30. The Roman Catholic Cathedral of St. Mary's is a stunning example of modern religious architecture. Designed by the architect Tange Kenzō, near the center of Tokyo, it was completed in 1964. Since that time its four imported bells have been heard for miles around calling the faithful to worship. The bright stainless-steel supports symbolize the light of Christ's message, and the hardness of the precast concrete walls symbolize that God is life's firmest foundation.

66 CHRISTIANITY AND JAPAN

31. International Christian University.

32. Meiji Gakuin.

33. Tsuda Juku Daigaku.

34. Tōyō Eiwa Jogakuin.

35. Rikkyō University.

36. Jōchi (Sophia) University.

37. Seishin Joshi Daigaku.

31–37. Meiji-era Christian evangelism left an enormous educational legacy. Pictured here are a few of the colleges and universities established under the auspices of Christian missions. International Christian University was built in 1952 as an interdenominational university dedicated to furthering international Christian education. Meiji Gakuin was established by the Presbyterian mission in 1886 and continues to build on the educational principles that were its foundation. Tsuda Juku Daigaku, a college for women, was opened in 1901 by Tsuda Umeko. Tōyō Eiwa Jogakuin was established in 1884 by the Canadian Methodist Martha J. Cartmell. It now includes a coeducational preschool, an elementary school, a junior high and high school, and a junior college for women. Rikkyō University (St. Paul's) was founded by the American Episcopal church in 1874. In addition to consistently having an enormously popular and winning baseball team, Rikkyō is the foremost college of the Episcopal tradition. Jōchi (Sophia) University continues the Catholic education that began there with its establishment in 1913. The university also publishes the respected scholarly journal *Monumenta Nipponica*. Sophia was founded by the Jesuits, who have always been diligent and effective in their missionary work in Japan. Seishin Joshi Gakuin and Seishin Joshi Daigaku (Sacred Heart) provide Catholic education for girls and young women from preschool through college. The schools of the Order of the Sacred Heart are known throughout the world for the strictness of their religious and academic principles.

Through cooperation between America and Britain, under the guidance of the British Anglican Bishop to Japan, Edward Bickersteth, two community missions, St. Andrew's and St. Hilda's, were established. St. Andrew's became the Episcopal Cathedral of Tokyo and originally had both foreign and Japanese members. Now the English-speaking community has its own church, St. Alban's, which is a Chapel of the Cathedral. The Anglican-Episcopal church has a heritage of able leadership and has been a church for both Japanese and foreign Christians.

Methodist Episcopal

A lesser known Christian band of the Meiji period was the Hirosaki Band in northern Honshu (Japan's main island). Honda Yoichi, who was a member of the Yokohama Band, had been sent to Yokohama to seek an English teacher for a local institution that educated the sons of samurai. In Yokohama he became a member of the Yokohama Band and joined the Christian church. There he met an American Methodist missionary named John Ing, who was on his way to China with his wife. Honda persuaded them to go north with him to his school and teach English. Honda and Ing baptized fifteen students soon after they began their mission. Ing's health forced him to return to America; Honda affiliated with the Methodist church and continued his work. Honda came from a distinguished samurai family, and two possible futures now lay before him. He could have become a politician and helped to build the new nation, but he decided to continue in the church. In 1888, he visited America. When he survived a bad accident in Pennsylvania he realized that he had been spared by God for a special purpose. He returned to Japan as a Methodist minister and eventually became the first bishop of the Methodist Episcopal church in Japan.

The Baptist Tradition

Jonathan Goble, the first Baptist to reach Japan, originally came to Japan on Perry's ship. He returned to America, became a Baptist minister, and came back to Japan in 1860. One characteristic of Baptist work was that it was geographically widespread in Japan. Around 1918, the dispersal of missionaries was organized into an East-Japan Convention (formerly Northern Baptist work) and a West-Japan Convention (including all Southern Baptist work). This two-part structure continued until 1941.

The Salvation Army

The Salvation Army in Japan was introduced from Britain in the 1890s, but it was the efforts of Yamamuro Gumpei (1872–1940), a student of Niijima's at Dōshisha, that established it on firm ground.

Yamamuro had decided to become a minister, but he concluded that conventional church life was too luxurious. He wanted to help people who were clearly in need. He became acquainted with a visiting deputation of the Salvation Army and saw that their efforts were directed toward the very people for whom he felt concern. He became a cadet in the Salvation Army and exemplified General Booth's chosen motto, "Work, work, work, and work again." Dedicating himself to the goals of the Salvation Army, he became editor of the Army newspaper *War Cry*. Yamamuro fought against almost every conceivable social problem—from slum poverty to prostitution. His work bequeathed to Japan a powerfully organized evangelistic and social reform group. The Salvation Army in Japan still ministers to the deprived members of society, and Yamamuro's evangelical book, *The Common People's Gospel,* has been reprinted over 500 times.

The Orthodox Church

What success the Orthodox church originally had was greatly due to the work of one man—Father Nicolai. This Russian missionary gave it an independent identity by separating the church from Russian politics. He arrived in Hakodate on 2 June 1861 as a chaplain to the Russian mission there. He returned to Russia in 1869–70 and secured status designating Japan as a mission of the Holy Synod of the Orthodox church. Nicolai stressed education for all church members: future clergy and believers as well as their children. In 1891, a great cathedral in classic Byzantine style was

The residence of August K. Reischauer, well-known Presbyterian missionary to Japan in the early twentieth century, when he was teaching at Meiji Gakuin, a missionary institution in Tokyo.

68 CHRISTIANITY AND JAPAN

opened in Tokyo. Nicolai was promoted to the rank of archbishop by the Holy Synod in 1906. He died in 1912, and left behind him a church of over 30,000 members in 266 congregations with 35 priests.

The Roman Catholic Church

The Church had never given up hope of recommencing the Japan mission. Much of its efforts towards renewal went into the building of churches. The first church was built in Yokohama in 1862, one in Nagasaki followed in 1865, and one in Kobe in 1870. A seminary was established for the training of priests in 1870. When the short period of persecution during the 1860s ended, an estimated 15,000 Japanese Catholics had returned to the discipline of the church.

The missionaries in this period were heavily supported by foreign funds. Between 1875 and 1890, the Catholic church established churches and missions in strategic centers of Japanese national life. After 1890, the problems of independence facing the Protestant churches began to trouble the Catholics. Growing Japanese feelings of national power and pride made the Catholic church recognize the need to train indigenous clergy. The problem of Japanese leadership in the Catholic community, however, has remained to the present day.

One continuing feature of the work of the Catholic church in Japan has been its enormous contribution to social welfare. Catholics founded the first institution for lepers at Gotemba in the late nineteenth century. Orphanages and homes for the aged were also established. Catholic activities today include mass communication—the production of a newspaper, broadcasting, and other forms of public witness.

The Religious Bodies Law

The development of the world's Christian churches has always been shaped by the domestic situations of various countries, and the rise of Japanese militarism and Japan's withdrawal from the League of Nations in 1933 were two events that had a major impact on Christian internationalism in the twentieth century. The government of Japan applied political pressure to the different churches, and a critical point was reached in 1939 when the Religious Bodies Law was passed. One provision of this law removed Shinto shrines from the category of religious institutions, thus exempting shrines, which were an integral part of the government's nationalistic structure, from the remaining provisions of the law.

The Christian churches were informed that to obtain legal recognition, a denomination must consist of fifty churches and at least 5,000 members. Various negotiations took place between the churches and, as a result, the United Church of Christ in Japan (Nihon Kirisuto Kyōdan) was established, uniting approximately thirty Protestant churches under Japanese leadership. Meeting at the Fujimichō Church on 24–25 June 1941, the participants produced a summary statement of the Christian faith, which was required by the Ministry of Education. The Kyōdan consisted of Japanese Synods, as well as those of the

The Salvation Army in Japan gathers around the collection kettle and receives contributions, a familiar sight the world over.

38. A brilliantly lit Christmas tree on a street in Ginza, Tokyo's premier shopping and entertainment district, attracts passersby to stop and enjoy the beauty of the decorations that accompany the celebration of the birth of Christ. While the commercial and convivial appeal of Christmas is currently the main appeal in Japan, the religious meaning, and the importance of the birth of Christ to Christian believers, is also conveyed through the joy-inspiring accompaniments to the celebration of Christmas.

39. In addition to ongoing traditional services, new and important Japanese contributions are being incorporated into Christianity. This can be clearly seen in the beautiful Christian Ikebana painstakingly arranged by Kyōko Grant. Mrs. Grant, who trained extensively in the meticulous Saga school of traditional Ikebana, has combined this discipline, rooted in Buddhism, with the spiritual content of the Christian faith and creates beautiful, symbolic flower arrangements to express Christian themes.

40–41. The continuing influence of the Christian church in Japan can be seen in these two pictures of Christian religious observances. From the baptism of a new, infant church member to participation at Sunday Services, the activities of Japan's Christian churches embrace the entire community. Infant baptism in Japan is rare, but is common in international Christian marriages. In Sunday services, strong emphasis is still placed on the sermon, and in Japan the Protestant church is best symbolized by the minister declaring God's word to His people. These church services were held at the Torizaka Church in Tokyo.

42. The graduation ceremony at International Christian University is the traditional occasion when graduating students are encouraged to take the Christian values from their educational environment out into the world of personal endeavor.

MAINSTREAM CHURCHES 71

Taiwan, Korea, and Manchuria missions. Its formation was consistent with long-held Japanese Christian desires for a united church, but the government had removed all choice from the churches and had made them vulnerable to government control.

Japan's war with China brought extreme hardship upon the whole nation, and by 1944 the war with the United States made Japanese church life almost impossible to maintain. The government had required that at all religious services the congregation bow toward the Imperial Palace (the residence of the emperor), hold a moment of silence for the war dead, and sing the Japanese National Anthem. The hymn book was censored to delete all references to God as judge or creator. In early 1945, the leader of the Kyōdan was called to the Ministry of Education for consultations on the implications that Christ's resurrection had for the status of the emperor. This confrontation, which would certainly have resulted in further Christian subjugation, was forestalled by Japan's surrender in August 1945.

Postwar Attitudes

The reconstruction of the Christian faith in the postwar period included rebuilding 500 war-ravaged churches. After the war, some of the participants in the Kyōdan resumed as independent denominations. Most of the mainstream Protestant groups remained to maintain the Kyōdan as the largest Protestant denomination. The fate of the Kyōdan, however, remains a matter of concern. The late 1960s radical student movement attacked it for complying with the military government during the war. Also, the existence of a Christian Pavilion at EXPO '70 in Osaka was condemned as collusion with government ambitions.

While to outside viewers, the contemporary Japanese government appears to be democratic, Japanese Christians have a more cautious perspective. They see more continuity with traditional Japanese politics than they like. Of course, they acknowledge the difference between the prewar military and the postwar civilian government. But their own past experiences have made them wary of the weaknesses within Japan's democratic institutions and the potential for exploitation of these weaknesses by the ambitious or irresponsible. Japanese Christians are sensitive to any sign of a return to authoritarian attitudes. Their concern is a vigilant watchdog in Japan today.

In 1887, Ishii Jūji, a Christian, gave up the study of medicine to establish the Okayama Orphanage. Housed in a rented Buddhist temple, Ishii's orphanage was an outstanding example of Christian social work. To learn a trade and help support the orphanage, the young men shown here are training to become barbers. The sign at the right gives the price for a shave and a haircut. In 1902 Ishii was decorated by the Japanese government in recognition of his work.

A FUTURE OF HOPE

Christ has yet many things to say unto us which we cannot bear until His Spirit has so enlarged our hearts that we are ready to learn from those whom we go forth to teach.

August Karl Reischauer

Common Characteristics of Church Life

What is Christianity like in present-day Japan? Who are today's Christians, how do they see themselves, and what are they attempting to achieve? The Christian church in Japan faces problems that are common to all denominations in every country. And it faces problems unique to its situation in Japan.

The baptism of infants and young children is unusual in Japan; rather, it is adults who are baptized, baptism being the result of a deliberate, conscious decision to become Christian. This decision still causes a great deal of soul-searching and may risk the loss of friends or mild harassment. After a person has made the decision to become a Christian, the baptism may often take place a year later. During that year, the convert will receive instruction on how to live a Christian life.

The way in which church members are distributed in Japan does not help to spread Christianity. Most are located in cities: Tokyo, which has 11 percent of Japan's population, is the home of 24 percent of Japan's Christians. Over 65 percent of all towns and 85 percent of all villages have no active Christian work of any kind whatsoever. This demographic distribution may reflect the fact that so many early Christian converts were people who became members of the business, bureaucratic, or academic middle classes in modern Japanese society, and these people lived in big cities. Furthermore, the continuing power of the family system has made evangelism very difficult in rural areas where participation in community customs and observances is almost unavoidable.

The congregations which have been formed in big cities have their own important features. For example, congregations exist on the basis of personal ties rather than on a geographical or territorial ministry as they do in Europe. The members may have been drawn to a certain church by personal links with the pastor or by his sermons. Consequently, the relationship is more a traditional one—the relationship between mentor and disciples rather than one between pastor and parishioners, and this results in the coming together of people of similar backgrounds. In this way Japanese congregations resemble American congregations where ethnic groups and people of common background more easily join together than people from the same community. Although Japanese churches have this characteristic in common with American churches, the pastor-church member relationship is very different, for the Japanese congregation is much more dependent upon its pastors. This is especially true in the case of the leaders of non-church Bible study groups. There the leader may exert tremendous influence upon his members' lives and careers.

For most Japanese men, the focus of their lives is not church membership of any kind, but the place where they work. Consequently, the place where most of their personal satisfaction is derived has no link with Christianity. Christian devotion can be an entirely private matter for Sundays, and an odd Sunday "off" from church attendance will usually solve any problem of conflict between work and worship. The difficulty of relating Christianity to activities other than Sunday ones can be difficult for the average salaried worker. More demanding Christian devotion is easier to pursue by those who are self-employed or who have more flexible weekly routines.

Japan's Christian churches have faced and overcome enormous financial problems. Japan has become economically powerful, and the churches have had to face the burdens of inflated land prices, huge building costs, and a lack of the big business patronage enjoyed by Shinto shrines and Buddhist temples. The early desire of the Japanese church for independence from foreign missionaries put a heavy burden on the small, struggling congregations. This burden was met by a very high level of giving which still continues. The Japanese church has battled for financial independence from its inception, too often placing an unfair burden upon its ministers, who have frequently had to (and

43–44. In recent years, Japan has received as honored guests two of the best known messengers of the major Christian traditions. The famous evangelist preacher Billy Graham conducted a crusade in Japan in 1967 and again in 1970. Both times huge crowds gathered to hear him. He is pictured here preaching at a meeting held in Kōrakuen, the baseball field of the Tokyo Giants, during his latest visit to Japan in 1980.

45–46. The Pope visited Japan in 1981 and attracted a large audience to this public religious meeting held under the banner "Pope is Hope" and conducted for the purpose of an exchange of ideas between the Pope and the Japanese people. Pope John Paul II was welcomed to Japan, during this same visit, by Emperor Hirohito.

74 CHRISTIANITY AND JAPAN

A FUTURE OF HOPE 75

still have to) hold outside full-time employment. These economic pressures limit the extent of rural mission work and ensure that students and white-collar workers still constitute the bulk of church membership. The churches' economic problems are still far from being solved.

The Christian Presence

The influence exerted by the Christian presence in Japan today is way out of proportion to its size. This creative 1-percent minority is trying to be the salt of the earth, enriching and improving the savor of the whole society. Three areas can be identified where the Christian presence is especially active: education, social conscience, and internationalism.

Christians today hold leading academic positions within every kind of Japanese educational institution, with Protestant groups taking education as their special concern. There are at present about thirty-eight Christian junior colleges, twenty-four Christian colleges, and nine major Christian universities. The Roman Catholic church maintains Jōchi (Sophia) University in Tokyo and other colleges in other parts of the country. Dōshisha University initially had Congregational funding, Meiji Gakuin University had a Presbyterian background, Rikkyō University (St. Paul's), had an Anglican-Episcopal background, and Aoyama Gakuin University and Kwansei Gakuin University had Methodist roots.

The establishment of the International Christian University in 1952 connects the present with this earlier heritage. ICU's first president, Yuasa Hachirō, was the son of the first elder of the Annaka Congregational Church founded by Niijima Jō, and had also previously been president of Dōshisha. When he died in 1981 at the age of 91, he was one of the last of the Meiji-born Christian leaders who had direct links with the first generation of the Protestant church in Japan.

The Christian educational influence extends to literature and the arts. Foremost among Christian authors are Shiina Rinzō (1911–73), Miura Shumon (1926–), and Sono Ayako (1931–). The novelist Endō Shūsaku (1923–), a devout Catholic, has produced numerous works dealing with Christian themes and their relation to Japanese society. Owing as much to their subject matter as to their lucid, unguarded style, Endō's novels are particularly accessible to an international readership while at the same time illuminating the indigenous Japanese psyche. Watanabe Sadao (1913–), a woodblock-print maker, has produced designs based on Biblical themes which have been widely acclaimed as giving Christian art a new form of expression. His work has completed the Japanization of sixteenth-century European Christian art that was stifled during the era of persecution.

Social Conscience

Christianity has always had a strong appeal in Japan because of its concern for human welfare: in return for faith it offers hope to the lonely, the bereaved, the outcast, and the exploited. By welcoming within the Christian fold those whom traditional society has shunned, Christianity has helped to nurture Japan's social conscience and make people aware of the injustices and sufferings in society and the concomitant moral obligation to correct them. The Christian presence has helped lead the struggle to strengthen Japan's commitment to social reform, and it continues to offer Japan an alternative to the deep-rooted Confucianist traditions of paternalistic benevolence and unquestioning loyalty.

Catholic and Protestant church members have both been active in areas of social concern, and the Catholic church has an impressive record. It has established more than 25 homes for the aged that house close to 1,500 elderly people, 35 hospitals that care for 5,000 patients, and 23 dispensaries that handle more than 500,000 consultations every year. The 60 Catholic orphanages and 113 day nurseries serve nearly 18,000 children. There are also 10 institutions for the handicapped providing care for about 800 patients. An emphasis on social work in Japan has been characteristic of the Catholic church since the arrival of the first Jesuits in the sixteenth century.

In addition to their extensive commitment to education, Protestants have also been engaged in similar social work. Concern about suicide inspired Christians to launch a service called *inochi no denwa* ("telephone lifeline"), which has had an impressive record since its inauguration in October 1971. This suicide-prevention service handles about 25,000 calls a year.

One outstanding example of Christian social work is the creation of the Keiyō Cultural Center in Chiba. A model Christian community center, the Keiyō Cultural Center serves a suburban town created for commuters who travel daily into Tokyo from Chiba. The center attempts to present a "servant church" within the dehumanizing atmosphere of an enormous housing complex where hundreds upon hundreds of identical tiny apartments in multistoried concrete buildings have been erected as close to each other as possible. Christianity is offered as a means of restoring humanity and mitigating alienation in this concrete jungle. As with similar complexes in Europe and the United States, many problems accompany such densely packed living situations, such as the existence of "key children" who return from school to empty houses because both parents are still at work. Nursery facilities for young mothers are important, as are other social agencies. But the mammoth size of these developments is beyond what any single Japanese church can handle. The Keiyō Cultural Center is an attempt to expand the limits of Christian care.

The Japanese Contribution to Christianity

Christianity and Japan have experienced both meeting and conflict. Where is there hope? Books galore today predict doom for the human race from nuclear destruction or from pollution and starvation. But two forces point toward the possibility of rising above the decay and chaos that surround us: the transcending hope of resurrection that is the heart of Christian faith and the spirit of endless renewal that is the root of Japanese civilization. Both are deeply and profoundly optimistic, both assert regeneration and the need for a deep spirituality to undergird it. In the union between these two there is hope.

Both Protestant and Catholic Christianity are changing. The most fundamental question is: can Christianity, which has been expressed since its inception in terms of Greek metaphysics, be expressed in any other way? Expressions like "substance" and "God in three persons" have classical roots that have no parallel in Oriental philosophy. While disagreements over these terms have wrenched the Western church in the past, the debate they have generated is meaningless to Chinese or Japanese ears. Shinto has no written scriptures and has not had need of them. Christianity has been sundered by words; Shinto endures without them. All persons are welcome at Shinto shrines, and Buddhism, which has many denominations, allows followers of other traditions or religions to take part in its ceremonies. Surely there can be a Christianity that remains Christian but which is not exclusive, dogmatic, or aggressive. Toward this goal, Japanese philosophy can offer several contributions to enrich Christianity.

Deep within Japanese culture flows a profound respect for spiritual discipline. Modern life has become soft and effete. Much of the illness of our age is caused by stress or excess. The Japanese, in recent years, have undertaken to renew their own ancient disciplines. Standing naked under frosty waterfalls, they attempt to become close to the world of nature. There has been a revival in pilgrimages by Japanese to spiritual places—to well-traveled sites in sacred mountain areas which date back hundreds of years. The need to bring order to life, to maintain a balance between society and nature, lies at the root of these undertakings.

Unlike Western asceticism, which glories in masochistic suffering, Japanese asceticism reveres discipline. This reverence is found in the martial arts, as well as in retreats dedicated to ascetic practices. Japanese businessmen, scholars, housewives, and workers testify to the therapeutic effects of a tough weekend program of spiritual exercises. They claim benefit not

An alternative to a Christianity atrophied by adherence to German categories of thought is offered by the Makuya (Tabernacle of Christ). Founded in 1948 by Teshima Ikurō (1910–73; see photo), Makuya broke away from the non-church movement to form a religion of complex Christian Pentacostalism. Makuya is a serious attempt to indigenize Christianity in Japan; it stresses immediate religious experience, Bible study, exegesis, and presents Christianity as a religion of healing. With 35,000 followers, Makuya has been described as the "third force" in Japanese Protestantism. Shown here is the worldwide yearly meeting of the Original Gospel Conference held in Niigata Prefecture, Myōkō-kōgen, in July of 1982.

only for their own sake but because such activities help them to cope with the stresses and problems of daily life.

Beyond acknowledging creation as the work of God, Christianity takes no official attitude toward the natural environment. Its views, which go as far back as the writings of St. Paul, reflect the prevailing climate of classical Stoicism: the world exists for the use of its rational members. Here is found one basis for seeing the world as something to be exploited. While the Old Testament does teach that man is the steward of God's creation, it also teaches that man should have dominion over it. Consequently, the role of steward received insufficient emphasis.

In striking contrast, Shinto holds nature to be divine. Great stones, majestic trees, and towering mountains are *kami*—beings and presences that inspire and engender reverence. In Western theology, mystical Celtic Christianity comes nearest to sharing the Shinto view. The ancient Scots and Irish saw God in their homes and fireplaces and in the lochs and glens. Medieval Catholicism saw the forest as the habitat of demons, the wilderness as a symbol of man's sinful nature. Protestant Christianity—its association with capitalism, the industrial revolution, and modern technological society—viewed as progress the clearing of forests and the building of factories. This Christianity has come, also, to be associated with a work ethic that many blame for the modern neurosis of alienation: alienation from home, society, and nature. Simply to visit a mountain shrine in Japan, to absorb the atmosphere of tall trees that have stood there for centuries, is to kno that with the loss of the mystical in our view of nature, we have lost one of our most precious assets.

Western Christianity, as we have seen, has done much to promote social concern on a broad scale. At the same time, it is closely associated with individualism. One's personal struggle with God, temptation, and individual worthiness as a human being often tends to obscure the significance religion might have for the health of the community as a whole. Japanese concerns, however, hinge on "groupism," the tendency among people at all levels of Japanese society to identify themselves as individuals with whatever it is they share—a neighborhood, a section within a company, a bowling team, an ancient rite or festival. Groupism at its worst can breed an uncompromising and destructive factionalism. But it is nevertheless capable of binding together people of decidedly different personalities, abilities, and needs as a single unit working for the common good, which ensures that benefits are equally distributed and that everybody's voice is heard. As many Western management experts have noted, the energy of a society can swiftly coalesce in a group. For example, the Japanese government's establishment of a consensus among diverse industries for selected types of growth was certainly one reason postwar Japan was able to marshal its limited resources so quickly and effectively.

By definition, Japanese group orientation tends to let the outcasts of society flounder. Public places in Japan, which cannot belong to any single "group," are often monstrously abused by littering, noisy, and careless crowds. Yet within its smaller, more manageable realms, the Japanese group soothes the affiliated individual in a warm bath of belonging and gives reassurance that no one is alone in the world. This is in some respects exactly the same sensation as is produced by a Christian's faith in God. Japanese groupism, then, may well offer some clues as to how a Christian's personal faith can function for the well-being of those around him whom he loves.

In Japan there are numerous possible new directions for the Christian spirit. If Christianity, at a time when it is struggling with problems of global scope, embraces these Japanese contributions, Christianity may again hear its own message of resurrection. A Christianity reborn with the strength of new insights will channel its massive energies and resources for the task ahead. It will surely become a world religion signifying hope.

The Christian Contribution to Japan

Just as the Christian religion can benefit from its meeting with Japan, the Christian presence in Japan contributes to three vital areas of Japanese life. It challenges Japan's rigid structures of human relations by offering mutual love as a basis for them; it staunchly supports Japanese peace movements; and it is a culturally embedded source of democratic ideals in the modern nation.

Christianity is helping to redefine the relationship between husband and wife in Japan. Japan's relatively low divorce rate does not necessarily mean an abundance of intimate, loving marriages. It more accurately denotes the fact that the basis for marriage in Japan is different from that of the West and is frequently pragmatic rather than romantic. There exist a good many marriages in Japan which were entered into in a Confucian spirit that to most Christians would seem cold.

The spiritualization of marriage has been one of Christianity's major achievements. Christian marriage is a sacred relationship, one that takes place between equals, and not a relationship of superior to subordinate as in Confucian ethics. The idea of entering into such a spiritual commitment based on profound love between two individuals is fairly new in Japan.

Indeed, the adoption in Japan of monogamous marriage is the result of Christian influence. The new Constitution emphasizes the rights of individuals, and mobility has gradually weakened the extended-family system while it has strengthened the nuclear family. All in all, the post–World War II environment has reinforced the idea of marriage based on spiritual commitment.

Not surprisingly, then, the Christian wedding ceremony is gaining popularity among young Japanese couples. Perhaps it is simply romanticism, for romance is often missing from the traditional Japanese marriage. To be sure, Japanese Christian churches take a dim view of the commercialization of the marriage ceremony and the proliferation of secular wedding "chapels" complete with crosses, ministers, sacred oaths, and hymn singing. But the fact that such wedding chapels are so successful is surely evidence of the need young Japanese have for a new basis for human relations. A spiritual marriage relationship has no basis in traditional Japanese values. The young are searching for a new husband-wife relationship that will make it a covenant between spiritual friends rather than a master-servant relationship. For the Christian church, this may be one vital challenge: to respond to their search as the religion of spiritual human relationships.

A major problem facing contemporary Japan is whether the nation can find a balance in its relationship with the modern world. Japan is, at one and the same time, an economic superpower ambivalent toward the rest of the world. From the viewpoint of other Eastern nations, Japan ranks with the industrialized nations of the West, while Western nations view Japan as remote and Oriental. Japan is respected and feared in both the West and Asia.

Though it is of course an oversimplification to say so, it seems sometimes that there are two forces struggling for the soul of Japan as it tries to plot its course in the modern world. There are those who wish Japan to move forward as a progressive, mature social democracy, applying economic rather than military strength, to help raise the living standards of developing nations and to be a force for stability and peace in Asia and beyond. But it must also be said that other forces continue to exist, voices advocating old solutions: a return to greater central control, a strengthened military complex, and the restoration of the prewar power of the emperor. Illustrating the conflict between these two forces is the controversy that arose in the summer of 1982 over the censorship of Japanese school history textbooks. The groups concerned with maintaining strong central control were in opposition to the Foreign Ministry, Christian groups, and international agencies. The latter saw that the school texts revised under instructions from the Ministry of Education, by softening the wording used to describe Japan's prewar activities, were attempting to minimize past Japanese military aggression and in so doing were damaging Japan's goodwill in Asia. The former argued for Japan's sovereignty: what was used to teach Japanese children in school should not be dictated by other governments, regardless of whether or not the material had been prepared with callous disregard for serious wounds yet unhealed.

This issue, like many others, indicates that beneath its modern surface Japan is struggling for a balance between embracing and withdrawing from the international community. This is a balance that island civilizations always find difficult to discover. It is not too much to say that Christianity in Japan and Japan's Christian friends can play an important role in determining which course shall be taken. Through the influence and presence described in this chapter, Christianity continues to generate social concern and a heightened awareness of international points of view.

There is no doubt that Japan's entry into the modern world was mediated in many ways by a supportive Christian presence, both Japanese and foreign. Christianity has in many ways helped Japan feel at home in the modern world. Christianity has provided insight and a broadened social vision, and it has helped Japan to understand what is expected of a responsible nation in a complex international age. It must continue to do so. We have seen that Christianity and Japan have much to offer each other; together they can join forces and become a source of hope. Christianity and the Japanese must ensure that hope is the outcome of Japan's Christian meeting.

A typical advertisement for a Christian-style wedding, including the ceremony, rental of bride's and groom's apparel, photographs, reception, and even the honeymoon. These all-in-one wedding packs are frowned on by the Christian churches in Japan but they demonstrate a desire on the part of young Japanese couples to enter into a marriage relationship begun on a new basis.

A FUTURE OF HOPE 79

BIBLIOGRAPHY

Christianity and Asian Civilization

Browne, Laurence F. *The Eclipse of Christianity in Asia.* Cambridge: Cambridge University Press, 1933.

Clark, Allen D. *History of the Korean Church.* Korea: Christian Literature Society of Korea, 1961.

Cohen, Paul A. "Christian Missions and Their Impact to 1900." In D. Twitchett and John K. Fairbank, eds., *The Cambridge History of China.* Vol. 10. London: Cambridge University Press, 1978.

Religion and Society in Japan

Anesaki, M. *History of Japanese Religion.* 1930. Reprint. Tokyo: Tuttle, 1963.

Bellah, R. N. *Tokugawa Religion: The Values of Pre-Industrial Japan.* New York: Free Press, 1957.

Benedict, Ruth. *The Chrysanthemum and the Sword.* Boston: Houghton Mifflin, 1946.

Ching, Julia. *Confucianism and Christianity: A Comparative Study.* Tokyo: Kodansha International, 1977.

Hall, J. W. *Japan: From Prehistory to Modern Times.* New York: Dell Publishing Co., 1968.

Nitobe, Inazo. *Bushido: The Soul of Japan.* Tokyo: Tuttle, 1969.

Nivison, D. S., and Wright, A. F., eds. *Confucianism in Action.* Stanford: Stanford University Press, 1959.

Spae, Joseph J. *Shinto Man.* Tokyo: Oriens Institute, 1972.

Suzuki, D. T. *Zen and Japanese Culture.* Princeton, N. J.: Princeton University Press, 1970.

Smith, R. J. *Ancestor Worship in Contemporary Japan.* Stanford: Stanford University Press, 1974.

The First Meeting

Boxer, C. R. *The Christian Century in Japan, 1549–1650.* Berkeley: University of California Press, 1951. Second edition, 1967.

Broderick, James. *Saint Francis Xavier.* London: Burns and Oates, 1958.

Cooper, Michael. *They Came to Japan.* Berkeley: University of California Press, 1965.

———, ed. *The Southern Barbarians.* Tokyo: Kodansha International, 1971.

Nagasaki: The Sea and the Cross

Cary, Otis. *A History of Christianity in Japan.* Vol. 1. 1909. Reprint. Tokyo: Tuttle, 1976.

Cooper, Michael. *Rodrigues the Interpreter: An Early Jesuit in Japan and China.* Tokyo: Weatherhill, 1974.

Hosono, Masanobu. *Nagasaki Prints and Early Copperplates.* Tokyo: Kodansha International, 1978.

Okamoto, Yoshitomo. *The Namban Art of Japan.* Tokyo: Weatherhill, 1972.

Persecution and the Hidden Christians

Bray, William D. "The Hidden Christians of Ikitsuki Island." *The Japan Quarterly* 26/2 (April 1960), pp. 76–84.

Elison, George. *Deus Destroyed: The Image of Christianity in Early Modern Japan.* Cambridge, Mass.: Harvard University Press, 1974.

Harrington, Ann M. "The *Kakure Kirishitan* and Their Place in Japan's Religious Tradition." *Japanese Journal of Religious Studies*, no. 4 (December 1980).

MacDonald, Alice E. "A Kirishitan Prayer Book-Catechism." *Japan Christian Quarterly* 28/1 (January 1962), pp. 55–60.

Meiji-Era Christian Missions

Blacker, Carmen. *The Japanese Enlightenment.* Cambridge: Cambridge University Press, 1969.

Cary, Otis. *A History of Christianity in Japan.* 1909. Vol. 2. Reprint. Tokyo: Tuttle, 1976.

Drummond, Richard. *A History of Christianity in Japan.* Grand Rapids, Mich.: William B. Eerdmans Publishing, 1971.

Duus, Peter. *The Rise of Modern Japan.* Boston: Houghton Mifflin, 1976.

Hardy, Arthur Scherburne, ed. *The Life and Letters of Joseph Hardy Neesima.* Boston: Houghton Mifflin, 1898.

Scheiner, Irwin. *Christian Converts and Social Protest in Meiji Japan.* Berkeley: University of California Press, 1970.

Chariots of Fire

Ariyoshi, Katsuhisa. *Dr. Masahisa Uemura: A Christian Leader.* Tokyo: Kyōbunkan, 1941.

Axling, William. *Kagawa.* New York: Harper Brothers, 1946.

Bacon, Alice M. *Japanese Girls and Women.* Boston and New York: Houghton Mifflin, 1891 and 1902.

Iglehart, Charles W. *A Century of Protestant Christianity in Japan.* Tokyo: Tuttle, 1959.

Kagawa, Toyohiko. *Christ and Japan.* London: S.C.M. Press, 1935.

Kitamori, Kazō. *Theology of the Pain of God.* Atlanta: John Knox Press, 1965.

Uchimura, Kanzo. *How I Became a Christian: Out of My Diary.* Tokyo: The Keiseisha, 1905.

Mainstream Churches

Griffis, William Eliot. *Hepburn of Japan.* Philadelphia: Westminster Press, 1913.

Jennes, Joseph. *A History of the Catholic Church in Japan.* Tokyo: The Committee of the Apostolate, 1959.

Johnson, Katherine. *In Our Time (1947–1957).* New York: Interboard Committee for Christian Work in Japan, 1959.

Kinoshita, Naoe. *Pillar of Fire.* Translated by Kenneth Strong. London: George Allen and Unwin, 1970.

Thomas, Winburn T. *Protestant Beginnings in Japan.* Tokyo: Tuttle, 1959.

A Future of Hope

Caldarola, Carlo. *Christianity: The Japanese Way.* Leiden: E. J. Brill, 1979.

Michalson, Carl. *Japanese Contributions to Christian Theology.* Philadelphia: The Westminster Press, 1960.

Phillips, James M. *From the Rising of the Sun: Christians and Society in Contemporary Japan.* New York: Orbis Books, 1981.

NAGASAKI: THE CHRISTIAN LEGACY

Until Luis de Almeida began missionary work there in 1567, Nagasaki was a small fishing village, just one of many sleepy harbor and inlet towns strewn throughout the Japanese islands. While Jesuits were interested in the souls of the villagers, the Portuguese traders were interested in the depth and safety of the natural harbor. An agreement was struck between the captains of the "black ships" and the Japanese lord within whose domain Nagasaki lay. Nagasaki became an international harbor in 1571, and in 1580 Nagasaki became the first piece of Japanese territory ceded to the Jesuit Order. From 1571 until the present day, Nagasaki has been the source by which much of European and Chinese culture made its way into Japan. Even during the days of Japan's self-imposed isolation—from about 1640 to the mid-1800s, when Dutch merchant activities were restricted to the nearby island of Deshima—Dutch and Chinese culture continued to seep into Nagasaki. And from Nagasaki it was transmitted throughout Japan. The flourishing scholarship in Japan based on Dutch science and medicine had its roots in Deshima and was in part responsible for undermining the foundation of the authoritarian Tokugawa regime and preparing the way for modernization. Since 1945, Nagasaki has been known the world over as the site of the second atomic bombing. Today this lovely harbor city represents the triumph of the human spirit over historical experience—it is an active Christian community as well as a community devoted to peace.

The large map to the right was charted in 1802. The island of Deshima, built in 1635 to house Dutch traders restricted from the Japanese mainland, can be seen a little way off the harbor coastline. The Chinese Compound, to which Chinese merchants and traders were confined, was built within the city of Nagasaki itself. Chinese, Japanese, and Dutch ships dot the harbor waters, indicating the bustle and activity that has been Nagasaki's hallmark since 1580. There is not one sign given on this map (trade with Portugal had long since been banned) to indicate that Nagasaki had ever been visited by, let alone given over to, the protection of the Jesuits. Long before 1802, every visible trace of Japan's Catholic encounter had been erased by the policies and military forces of first Toyotomi Hideyoshi and then the Tokugawa government.

Despite all efforts to the contrary, much of Nagasaki's Catholic Century does remain, side by side with relics from the Meiji period when foreigners and missionaries could once again live freely in the city. Together these landmarks, shown on the modern map (inset left), tell the story of Nagasaki's varied and dramatic history.

1. The Ōura Church, built by the Jesuits in around 1571, is the oldest Western-style building in Japan. It is known in Nagasaki as the "church of the 26 martyrs," as it has long been associated with the first Catholics martyred in Japan in 1597.

2. The garden and residence of Thomas Glover, a prosperous merchant of the Meiji period, make up just one of the Meiji-period houses and gardens that still exist in Nagasaki. Puccini's opera *Madama Butterfly* was based on the romantic story of Glover's life.